The SHADOW FLAMES of

ULURU

Book ONE in the CHAOS DOWN UNDER Series

MATT B. BRODIE

THE SHADOW FLAMES OF ULURU

Book ONE in the CHAOS DOWN UNDER Series

Matt B. Brodie

ISBN-13: 978-0692212974

ISBN-10: 0692212973

Christian Publishing House

Cambridge, Ohio

THE SHADOW FLAMES OF ULURU: Book ONE in the CHAOS DOWN UNDER Series

Matt Brodie is to be identified as the author of this work.

Editor: Gina Burgess

Christian Publishing House
Professional Christian Publishing of the Good News

Acknowledgements

I would first like start off by thanking my Lord Jesus for giving me the inspiration and drive to write this novel. It is with His intervention that this book made it to print.

I also want to thank my family for being supportive and encouraging me to succeed in whatever I do. I thank my brother for helping to reveal the gem when it was only a seedling. The Biblical aspects of the novel, I give credit to my grandmother.

A special thanks to Rogan Swift, a good friend, who helped polish and revise the early stages of the prose. After many hours of laughter and discussion, over equivocal meanings of phrases and adding description where needed, we managed to produce a read that was both compelling and vivid before the book was sent it to the editor.

I want to the thank Gina Burgess, who took the time to edit the novel for publication. She helped iron out the wrinkles and really brought this book to all it could be.

Lastly, I want to thank the owner of Christian Publishing House for taking on this novel to share the Good News of the Gospels.

Book 1

The horizon darkens
And blazes with rage.
Death smiles with eyes of green.
To my descendants I pass the torch.

CHAPTER 1 An Omen of Shadows

AMBER

THE ONCE QUIET STREETS of my hometown now thunders with the screams of people fleeing for their lives from packs of kangaroo-like dogs. From the front, they look like coyotes, but from the belly back, you could mistake them for a kangaroo. Brown stripes slice the tan fur of their hides along their backs similar to tiger stripes, though the camouflage stripes seem to fade whenever they change direction. Yet, their eyes are phantom-green and blaze with unquenchable vengeance against humanity: vengeance for hunting them down through the centuries. I've seen them before, but their name evades me. They came out of nowhere. Yesterday everyone's life was normal, but today chaos and panic abounds.

I walk amid the chaos while a gentle breeze caresses my face with my cedar-red hair. The winter sun warms me as it rises into an azure sky. No one notices me. Everyone flees from the dogs. I'm invisible. A ghost. Some even run through me.

Then one of the dogs looks at me, and time stops as we lock eyes. Then he yawns, his jaw opens like a croc's as he paces before me. Suddenly, he rushes me, and leaps into the air with jaws gaping, and threatening to rip me to shreds.

To save my skin, I scramble over a low fence cutting through a neighbor's yard. I don't think they are going to care if some schoolie trespasses through their yard, trampling a few blades of grass or flowers. I mean, would you care about flowers if dogs supposed to be extinct are overrunning the streets? Me, neither.

Behind me, while I stand in a small green at the corner of Essex Road and Ward Street, echo the screams of my peers. I instinctively turn for home. The street suddenly dead-ends where my house once stood, and in its place is a wall of black flames that claw at the heavens. The dogs burst from the fire. I turn to watch them disappear into the streets as they leap at those driving to work, or maul my fellow classmates. I run from the fires. Now, I know running back into the streets isn't the brightest thing to do, but with my house out of the picture where else *can* I go?

I decide to take refuge in my school, in a classroom mind you, since all our hallways are outside, but no one sees me at the door. I knock on it, and still no one notices. I open the door and see they continue to hide from the chaos.

Suddenly, the wind turns violent threatening to rip the door from it's hinges. I struggle with it, finally wrenching it from the wind's clutches. It bangs shut. Safe inside the room I glance around. Everyone is texting or cowering at desks, but I feel another presence in the classroom, a presence I know I felt before. Looking around again, I see the silhouette of a boy standing at the door beside me. I study him, wondering where I saw him before. Then one of the dogs jumps at the door, interrupting my thoughts, and my gaze turns from it to the black flames (I'll call them Shadow Flames) gathering on the horizon. A Wagiman chant resonates in my ears. I'm half Wagiman (an indigenous tribe whose language is still spoken), so I can make out some of the chant.

"Shadow rises. Light will fall," I hear the phrases repeating.

The Shadow Flames' tongues of black fire swirl up into the charcoal skull of one of the dogs that terrorize the citizens of Indooroopilly. The horns of a ram twist from the skull filled with the dark fire. In the sockets, the same green eyes blaze like stars. The skull's jaw hangs open as the Shadow Flames surge toward me churning like the shock wave of a nuclear bomb shattering the glass. I scream in horror as the concussion tosses my body across the room.

I am up from my bed like a catapult, screaming. Then I glance around the room. Sweat drenches my sheets, and my blood throbs in my temples.

"It was only a nightmare," I tell myself. "You're safe. That wasn't real."

I expect my parents to barge through the door any second because I roused them, but no one comes.

Thinking about the nightmare shoots a cringe through my body. Those eyes still flash about my room whenever I blink. The screams of people ring in my ears as well, and the corners of the room remind me of the Shadow Flames. Staring at the ceiling, I pray the nightmare will not return as soon as I close my eyes.

A soft knock on my door resonates through the room, jolting me. I glance at my alarm: one forty in the morning. I moan longing for whoever is at the door to just rack off, but the knocking persists.

"What?" I whine half asleep.

"Amb, I need to speak with you." Michael, my fraternal twin rasps.

Throwing back the covers, a cool winter draft seeps through my pyjamas. I drag myself to the door. Michael enters, a concerned expression on his face. He sits on my bed while I crawl back under my sheets.

"What do ya want?" I ask. "It's one in the morning, Mike."

"I had the most horrific nightmare," he yawns, half asleep.

He probably wants to talk about it, so I let him, half expecting some drawn out explanation of the weird whatevers in his dream.

"Okay... and you want to discuss it or something?"

"It was weird. I was walking to school when thylacine chased our schoolies through the streets. Some leapt on cars of people going to work. So, I take refuge in the school and turn around to see these black flames gathering into

11

the skull of a thylacine on the horizon. I hear it scream, and then the flames surge forward like a tsunami engulfing our hometown of Indooroopilly."

I want to kick him out. We had the same dream! This crosses the line of bizarre. "I dreamed the exact same thing just a few minutes ago."

In the dim light, I see his puzzled stare. "Pull the other one, Amb! Even twins don't have the same dreams unless…"

"Unless?"

"Unless it was meant to be."

"Well, Mike, I'm telling you, I had the same dream. You can choose to believe me, or not. I also heard this Wagiman chant."

"I did, too, so we did have the same dream. What do you reckon it means?" he inquires.

"Do I look like a dream interpreter to you?" He has no answer. "Sorry Mike, it's way too early for this. You mind if we go back to bed and catch a few more winks?"

He nods wishing me pleasant dreams and walks out. I wish him the same.

"By the way, Mike, what did you say those dogs were called again?"

"Thylacine, but get this. They were declared extinct in 1936, and we had a dream about them today."

Only Mike would know something like that. I smile, but he doesn't see it. He wishes me good-night and closes my door.

"Good-night, Mike." I yawn to myself, resting my head on my pillow.

CHAPTER 2 Eve of Destiny

AMBER

SIX-FORTY-FIVE MY ALARM CHIRPS and I slap the snooze button, sprawling out under the covers.

Then the door opens, and the light flickers on, flooding my room with its brilliance. "Rise and shine, Princess," says my Dad, closing my door.

I throw my pillow over my head dousing the light. A child's cry drifts to my ears on a gentle breeze. The eerie cry rouses me. Alert, I rush to the window and see a thylacine sniffing about our front yard, but when I rub my eyes, he vanishes. Shrugging my shoulders, I dress.

What to wear? Capris. That'll do. I pull a pair of white Capris and a blue sweater from my dresser, and draw my hair back with a hair band.

Exiting my room, I look out the sliding door to our balcony-patio. A lounge chair tempts me to sit on it to soak in the first rays of the sun. It invites me to forget about the morning routine for a few minutes. In the neighbor's yard, the sun glints through a palm tree. My hometown spreads out under the sun's rays. "G'day, Indooroopilly," I say to the world at large, stretching.

Morning-zombie Michael lumbers from his room in blue plaid pajama bottoms. Pale freckles dapple his nose and cheeks. His red hair is the aftermath of Blanket War Twelve, and his brown eyes droop with his longing to return to bed.

Then there's his three-millimetre spacer. The piece of jewelry suits him. However, it created such uproar between my oldies; I swear they fought about it daily. Mind you, it was not one of the scream-at-each-other-squabbles. The argument was calm, but intense. Dad told Mum to let him be, and that it wasn't harming anyone. Mum in turn reminded him the earring symbolized rebellion, which was not something we strived for in this household. Ironic how Mum, of all people, would be talking about rebellious behavior. She used to be the girl who would party and drink until she was as full as a goog! She claims it was a past life, a phase. Dad, on the other hand, I can see as a biker back in the day.

It's been three weeks since my brother started wearing the spacer, and I secretly think the spacer has grown on Mum even though she denies it.

As Michael walks to the bathroom, I feel sympathetic about the slight limp in his walk. We take Taekwondo lessons, and one time he landed wrong. The entire class heard the crack. Michael was on the floor nearly in tears with his ankle twisted sideways. The doctor said he tore the tendons, and it has left him limping ever since.

I walk downstairs, and on the kitchen bench rests two pieces of toast with Vegemite spread on them. The note reads (in Dad's handwriting) "Enjoy, Princess."

I ignore the plate and rummage through the pantry for corn flakes. In case you don't know what Vegemite is, it is our variation of Marmite, which originated in Britain. It's a by-product of manufacturing beer. Most Aussies love the thick, dark brown paste. Me? I gag at the smell of it. I'm not, as the song says, "a happy little Vegemite."So I pour milk into my bowl of cereal as my brother joins the living. He looks at the toast on the bench.

"May I?"

"Knock your socks off, I'm not eating it."

He bites the corner off the toast and sits down across from me.

"So what do you think?"

"I don't want to talk about that." I snap.

"All right, no need to get off your bike, Amb, I was just saying."

"Mike, drop it, please."

My brother takes the plate to the computer, and plops down in the chair.

"What're you doing?" I ask. "School starts in half an hour."

"I know, but I just thought I'd look up those dogs on the Tasmanian coat o' arms."

I walk over, eating my cereal. "Anything?"

"Gimme a sec, will ya? I just started."

He pulls up the Internet searching for the coat of arms. It is the first thing we see. Two of the dogs from last night's dream stand on their hind legs, with their forepaws holding the shield. He scrolls down the page, where it describes the coat of arms.

"Here. Thylacine." He types thylacine into the browser and a grainy image of the beast with its jaw agape stares back at us. Haunting. I can almost hear it scream. The scream comes again. We exchange glances, and I pray my gut is wrong.

As soon as we exit our door, chaos like in our dream abounds. I hear yips and screams, and recognize the sound. Thylacine. The nightmare flashes through my mind, and Michael takes off running.

"Where are you going? Michael! Urh!" I take off after him.

My brother cuts through the small green on the corner of Essex Road and Ward Street, two thylacines blindside us, knocking us to the ground. Unlike the ones I saw in my dream, these have brown, kangaroo-like eyes. I use the only weapons I have to fend off the beasts: my feet. Thrashing, I kick them in the stomachs. Suddenly, two figures blot out the sun, and one raises a club to the heavens. I close my eyes and hear a loud *thwack* then the thylacines are yelping in retreat. I'm spared from the horrific sensation of being disemboweled, but I dare not move.

My eyes only open when I hear a calming, musical voice, "It's all right children. The danger has passed."

I prop myself up with my hands checking that the voice spoke truth. I stand up, and take a moment to brush off all the sand and gravel stuck to my legs and backside. I see my hair band, and stoop to pick it up. Michael bounds to his feet in a single movement. Mike always manages to pull off feats like that. I'm relieved he's safe.

The woman smiles at us while the man stares with a stern expression. Both wear very little clothing. The man is muscular and toned. He's wearing nothing more than a red vest and a cloth covering his... area. He has a sash holding a boomerang, two daggers, and a few pouches sown into the sash. A simple band of cloth wraps his forehead. Ashen hair is in high contrast with his round and flat cinnamon face. He holds a spear in his right hand. The woman wears a modest, knee length skirt and a band brassiere, but I see her naval. She wears leather thongs on her feet and a braided tiara with the colors of mahogany, crimson and sea blue atop a frizzy mop of soot-colored hair. She too wears a dagger and a boomerang at her waist.

"Thanks." I say. "We'd have been an easy meal."

"You're welcome, children."

I suddenly realize that they were not with us when we were running from the beasts, and I didn't see them in the crowds either. "How did you two... just, you know, " the man cuts me off.

"That not clear? I throw my buran at them." He says, removing his boomerang from his sash.

"No, that's not what I meant. How did you get *here?*"

"That not important. Evil is overrunning city, and we must act."

"So I've noticed," I mutter.

"You speak of the dogs? No, they are not the threat. I refer to *Lawurl Guda*, on horizon."

Shadow Fire? I freeze, hesitant to turn around. Michael does, and I hear him start to speak.

Please don't be there! Please don't be there! Please don't be there!

I close my eyes and turn around. Opening them, I see what I prayed not to see. The Shadow Flames. Horror stricken, I turn away.

"You have seen these events, too? Uli Marawara must have given you similar vision then."

Michael turns around, casting a puzzled glance at the man's sudden words. "Time out. Who are you, and who is this Uli bloke?"

"I am Maliu Koamu, and this is my wife Qi. Uli was renowned shaman in our tribe many suns ago. He gave me a vision. In it, he say, 'Maliu, find my family'. And he showed me you two."

"Charmed. Well, I'm Amber and this is my brother Michael, and we don't know of any Uli-man."

"He say you might say that, and he say to tell you that he was your grandfather.

"So that makes you our uncle or something?"

"No. I am not family. Amber and Michael what you saw last night begins. You tell me Uli gave you vision about events too?"

I roll my eyes, saying, "We had a nightmare."

"Did Uli give you this nightmare? Because then he must have given me same nightmare, but in mine, he tell me to tell you, you must destroy evil behind *Lawurl Guda*."

This keeps getting better. First, we're given nightmares by a grandfather we've never heard of, and now he's telling us we have to save the world! What next? We have to do it before noon, or it'll explode?

I bite my finger, just to make sure I'm not having another wild dream.

My gaze shifts to my brother. Knowing him so well, I observe his deep-thinking pose. His noggin sparks and smoke pours from his ears. "Hold on. Why come to us? Why don't you just deal with the Shadow Flames yourself? Or better yet, go to some kind of authority position or something?"

"You call *Lawurl Guda*, Shadow Flames? Then I will call them same thing. Shadow Flames cannot be seen by City Fellas. Amber and Michael, you are special. Uli say that because you his grandchildren, you can stop the Evil."

Well, that clears up a host of questions!

As far as the do-it-yourself aspect, Malui and his wife are too old. I take a second glance at them. Maliu has to be at least sixty, so perhaps he *had* thought of doing it himself and knew he couldn't.

Michael and I look them full in the face. I brush a stray lock of hair behind my ear. "All this seems so sudden. Can we at least plan a little first?"

"No time. You must go now."

"Why? What's so dire that demands our immediate attention? All we want to do is go home and grab a few things."

A growl interrupts Maliu's response. A lone thylacine walks onto the green. The beast snarls, and then leaps for Michael and me. Maliu steps in front of us, and the beast pins him to the ground. As it snaps at him, he holds it at bay with his spear.

"Qi, take Amber and Michael to our daughter! Get them out of here!"

Qi takes us by the hand, but I wrench myself free and run. Michael follows. We run without thinking about direction, it doesn't matter where. We end up at Indooroopilly State High, or Indro as it's called. Out of breath, Michael and I walk into school. I reckon it'll be safer indoors.

The events of this morning, still pound in my head, and they are all I can think about, so I excuse myself from my class and walk to the washroom. There I break down crying. Maliu saved my life, and I told him off.

What if he didn't come to my aid? I'd be... don't think about it! I had to assure myself, *You would have pulled through somehow.*

After five minutes, I gather myself together, and walk back to class. Taking my seat, my mind still is racing.

What if Maliu is telling the truth? These Shadow Flames could be a time bomb. No, Maliu can't be telling the truth. He's got kangaroos loose in the top paddock. A delusional aborigine. The dream we had last night was only a dream. We're still safe. There are no Shadow Flames. The thoughts help, but I know I'm only lying to myself. Everything I dreamed happened (except the part where Maliu saves me, I didn't dream that).

Mr. Tanner calls on me for an answer to a question. I ask, "Can you repeat that?"

"I know I can be excruciatingly boring Miss Hauksby," the class laughs, "but please try to stay with us. I asked you what year was this country colonized?"

All eyes fall on me. I put my head down in my arms, trying to hide my embarrassment.

Fortunately, the bell rings, and I'm able to walk to my locker with the crowd. I open the locker, cradling my books in one arm.

"How ya goin', Hauksby," a schoolie says.

My books drop to the floor, thankfully none land on my foot. Travis Fukushima, the bloke who startled me, bends to help me pick them up. His black hair is spiked at the forehead and highlighted blond. He wears a neon red T-shirt, jeans and sandals.

"Thanks," I say. "I gotta run."

He grasps my wrist. "Hauksby wait. I want to know one thing, that's all."

I brush strands of hair out of my face. "Wait, I know this one. You wanna know why I hate blokes so much, right?"

Travis shakes his head. "No, I wanted to know if you noticed anything strange as you were walking to school this morning."

"If by strange you mean extinct animals running rampant in the streets then yes, I have."

"What do you think it means?"

"Dunno. Don't care at the moment. See ya around, Travis."

Travis grabs my arm and turns me around. I wrench my elbow from his grip, "You mind? I have Taekwondo at four and I need to get home to get ready."

"You're going back out? Into that?" His tone is incredulous.

"Look, the way I see it, those thylacines can return to extinction. And I'm not going to let some demon stand in my path, altering my future!"

"I'm a demon to you?"

I suddenly realize how he could interpret my words like that, so I do a bit of damage control. "That's not what I meant. I've just had... a really weird morning, okay?"

"Yeah, it's strange out there."

Not what I meant either, but all right. I let it go.

I see Michael walking down the hall toward me. He body-checks a friend into his locker. The two roughhouse for a little. Then Michael continues walking like nothing happened. He nods to some of the girls watching the scrap. They turn to each other, giggling. I place my hand on my hips when he sees me.

He forestalls my greeting and says, "There you are. Quit being a flirt and let's go."

I wasn't being a flirt. I was trying to get rid of this bloke. I give him a withering look, and he gets the message, I reckon.

"We gotta run, Travis, but we'll see you around," my brother says.

Travis nods, walking off.

"Mind telling me what that was about?" His tone is playful, instigating.

"You know I don't flirt, Mike. Travis just wanted to talk about the events of this morning."

"You told him about the Shadow Flames?"

"Of course not! The bloke would think I have kangaroos loose in the top paddock! I mean, wouldn't you?"

"Hard to say with all that's been happening. I overheard a few schoolies discussing how they saw thylacine just disappear as though they were walking through a wall. Some said they saw cars do the same thing and then reappear half way down the street, and then careen into oncoming traffic. Roads, freeways, trains. Amb, the entire system is down!"

I bit my lip. We may be dealing with this threat, whether I liked it or not.

Taekwondo is cancelled because of the chaos, so we spend the evening doing homework. Well, I do. Michael surfs the web for anything on the Shadow Flames. I stay in the uniform though, since it is more comfortable than what I wore to school.

At around seven, someone raps on our door. I answer it. Three guesses whom. Travis? Dad? Maliu and his wife. Fantastic! Now he's stalking us. Though, I *am* amazed he survived his conflict with that thylacine, I still bar the way.

"What're you doing here?"

"You and your brother, must leave tonight."

"We're not going. Find some other schoolies to go on your quest. I'm sure Uli has many other children who are just as capable as we are. Michael and I aren't interested."

Mum steps from the dining room wearing a housecoat. "Who might you be?" She asks politely, though I catch an edge in her tone.

"Sorry to disturb. Must address pressing matters." Maliu explains his reasons for showing up so late.

He can make all the reasons he wants to, I'm still not going. Mum on the other hand, engages him. "And you are?"

"Maliu Koamu. I spoke with Amber and Michael about Evil Spirit plaguing city this morning. May we come in?"

Mum raises an eyebrow. "What do you want with my children?"

"You have seen Shadow Flames on the horizon, yes? That is why I come. I come to discuss with you. I would prefer it be done inside so we do not attract attention."

Mum hesitates. I reckon she's contemplating whether to let this couple in then I see her nod. She invites them into the living room. As she passes me, I scowl. Mum beckons them to the couch, but they choose to sit on the floor, then Mum offers them a drink. They request water. My eyes narrow when

Mum points me to the couch. Why is she being hospitable? I want these two out! Now!

Qi looks me over. "Do you wear night clothes?"

I bury my face in a pillow, ignoring her.

Mum returns with a tray in her hands. On it are the waters, a lemonade, and a glass of wine, which I assume is for her. She serves our guests first, then hands me the lemonade. She sits down in the Cube and Maliu begins. He asks if everyone is present.

"My brother isn't. If you like I can go grab him."

I intend to walk upstairs, hit the sack, and let Mum coax the Ko-whatever's out. That plan flops when Michael trudges into the room wearing pajama bottoms and rubbing his eyes. I cast him a look, but he doesn't notice and sits down beside me on the couch.

"This is all?" Maliu asks.

Mum sips her wine then tells Maliu our father works late tonight. Maliu nods then opens with a summary of the morning. He informs us that he spent the afternoon studying the Shadow Flames, and he has good news and bad news about it.

The good news *and* bad news is the fires remain idle. For me, the Shadow Flames just sitting there is great news! It means I don't have to deal with the threat. He expands on his claims. "Amber, must understand. Evil Spirit plans as we sit. Shadow Flames are stagnant yes. Why? How long? Until I know more, assume worst. For the moment, Shadow Flames present no threat. So news both bad and good.

"Must delay no more. Two of you must find source of flames, find out all you can. Then with the knowing you have, you must extinguish fire, destroy Evil Spirit."

Michael jumps to his feet, rubs his hands together. With a glower I make him sit again then my gaze shifts to Mum. She nervously sips her wine. The glass trembles in her hand, so she sets it down not to spill it all over the armchair, and I can tell the thought of losing us is bordering on unbearable for her. She doesn't believe this magician, does she?

Mum sighs. I stand corrected. "You asked if I have seen these Shadow Flames. I have, and I was hesitant to take Amber and Michael to their Taekwondo class then we found out it was cancelled. But, I want to know, why are my children the only ones who know about these Shadow Flames? Surely, there are others who know about them and can see them. It's late and *if* my children are the only ones then they should prepare for this, right?"

"Miss, blue sky shrouds flames. No City Fella see it. You and children can, because you have blood of Uli Marawara, and children have received vision from Uli"

"How do you know about Uli? And what vision are you referring to?" How does *Mum* know about Uli?

"He was a shaman of my tribe, and when he was young he, "

"Let me guess, he sealed the Evil Spirit, but forgot one small detail and now it's back with a vengeance. Right?"

"No. In vision Uli give me, he show me when he young fella, he came across an opal. In the core was a black flame. He saw man mining opal, too. The stone cracked before him and he fled. Now, opal is broken. Shadow is free. What Uli neglected to do, you and brother must do, or Australia plunge into darkness." He addresses my mother. "He give children premonition of events today. And shadows are still. Cannot say for how long, and that is why you must go now."

"We're still not going. Find someone else." I say.

"No one else. You two are only ones."

"I reckon, you just don't want to find anyone else Maliu!"

"Can't you give us a little more time to prepare at least?" Michael asks. I really, wish he would not engage this egghead.

"My son makes a valid point. If my children are, as you say, the only ones who can do this then," Mum scolds, "either you give us more time to prepare, or I call the authorities to have you locked up!"

Maliu closes his eyes. "Uli, your grandfather, predicted this. He said 'My children who receive the vision of *Lawurl Guda*, must leave within one moon, so they may defeat the demon and lift the veil'. One moon means they leave tonight or they will not succeed."

I roll my eyes, and though I loathe the idea of being related to a witch doctor that spent his days groping about the Outback, I cannot deny the facts: Mum is half aborigine, so it is our ill fate to take on this task.

Maliu stands. We gather our belongings, and I head to the carport to retrieve our hiking bags and sleeping sacks. I also take the family's hunting knife from the wall. Taking the knapsacks inside, I toss one to my twin. Then we head upstairs to pack.

"Are you ready, Amber, Michael?" Maliu calls from the bottom of the stairs.

"As I'll ever be. Let's just get this over with."

Maliu ushers us to Jack Speare Park, and there we wait.

CHAPTER 3 The Shadow Welcome Committee

MICHAEL

OVERHEAD, AMBER AND I HEAR the choppy whir of a helicopter. I look up squinting at the landing lights. The craft hovers over the park for a moment then lands. The pilot shuts off the engine, and the rotors slow to a stop then the blades droop. On the side of the shell I make out Joey-242.

A stocky woman in her late teens or early twenties steps out of the cockpit. In the city light, I notice she wears a pair of khaki pants and a jean jacket, which she has buttoned up. Rightly so, since the night is a little nippy. She and Amber have the right idea, while I chose a T-shirt and jeans. I instinctively rub my arms, warming them slightly. Her black hair is straightened and tied back in a ponytail. The woman introduces herself as Gali.

Being polite, Amber and I return the greeting. I notice the family resemblance between her and Maliu.

Gali sips a beverage from a large, metal canteen. Considering the late hour, and that she has to fly us to wherever our drop off point is, I assume it's a caffeinated beverage of some kind. She sets the canteen in the cockpit and opens a small cargo hold on the side of the body. Gali insists on loading it, so we let her.

"You tykes are saving Oz. It's the least I can do," she says.

Amber doesn't seem to care either way. She just wants to get this quest over and done with (she made that apparent back in the living room). And I reckon by the way she flicks her bangs out of her face and taps her foot that she still dreads the idea of saving Australia. So trying to take her mind off the quest, I decide to be a gentleman and open the door for my sister, but she doesn't seem to notice. Instead, she just clambers in and slumps into the chair turning her gaze to the window.

Well, at least I tried. No harm in that. The worst she could have done was glare at me, I guess. I follow her in as Gali closes and locks the cargo hold. Maliu wishes us luck and slides the door shut.

"Wait Maliu, where is the source of the Shadow Flames?" Too late the door is closed and he is walking away.

Thankfully, Gali hears my question and answers it for me as she pitches herself into the cockpit then pulls the door closed in one smooth motion. "My father reckons the source is somewhere in the Outback since he went to the coast today and did not see them there." She locks the door.

Somewhere in the Outback. Wouldn't it be easier if Gali flew us to the source? So I ask.

"It would yes, it's just that there have been many reports of planes going down over the Outback recently, and on top of that my fuel will just get us over the Great Dividing Range. I've also got an appointment with a journalist in Adelaide. Sorry mate."

Part way is better than walking from Indooroopilly, so I sit back in my seat.

Gali flips a few switches, one of which lights up everything on the instrument panel so she could see. She flips on the cabin lights, and the shadows flee in an instant. Seating is for seven people. The leather upholstery is a new, gleaming bar of chocolate, and the floor is free of litter. White panels of the interior contrast with their black frames. The two chairs before us appear to swivel. I'm guessing it is a revitalized cabin,

I turn my attention to the front, recognizing the warning lights, the search light and a few others. Ten at the most and part of me wants to know what all of them do, but I am too zonked to ask.

Keys and other knick-knacks jingle and clatter around while Gali fishes through a glove compartment. Finding what she was looking for, she lobs us each a pouch full of ruler length double-edged blades. I take one out studying it. The blade has a small notch cut into the tang as if to clip into something else. I apply a bit of pressure to the tip and the blade bends slightly. Steel most likely. I begin to contemplate uses for the blades. Projectiles, utensils (well, maybe not that one), carving tools.

"And these are for?" Amber inquires a slight edge to her tone.

Gali motions for her to look under the seat as she turns on the floor lights. My sister pulls out two pairs of gauntlets. Brass encases the wrists and knuckles of tanned, leather gloves, and houses a guard with a slit cut in it for the blades. At first glance, they look like dead weights, but surprisingly turn out to weigh about two sticks of butter. Chiseled into the top of the wrist guard is this stanza:

Those who hope in the Light

Will renew their strength.

They will soar on wings

Like eagles.

I study the verses to the stanza. They ring in my mind, but I cannot remember where I heard them, so I put the thought from my mind, and turn my attention to assembling the weapon (assuming everything works in harmony).

Gali offers to show us how to use the weapons, so I give her one of mine. They are simple. Load the blade flat into the slot. Point at the target, ball a fist to shoot. The firing mechanism, attached to a chain, is released by the thumb. Probably a good idea when shaking hands with someone.

"You two can practice on a tree in the Outback tomorrow," says Gali. "It'll take that long to get where my father instructed me to drop you off."

Then, fiddling with a few switches, we hear a soft beeping noise. Gali turns it off. She flips switches multiple times. Presses the same buttons twice. She is testing functions to make certain everything works as it should. Gali takes ten minutes to go through all the procedures, so by the time she fires the Joey-242 up it's nine in the evening.

Amber jabs my arm. "Rise and shine, wombat." A playful grin creases her lips. Her sudden change in mood is confusing. Yesterday she was resenting this quest, and now she isn't? What's up with that?

"Yes, Mike, I still dislike the idea of being out here. In fact, I would much rather be listening to Mr. Marrket talk about the particle theory right now."

I may be a bookworm when it comes to the sciences and math, but Mr. Marrket is the most monotone teacher at Indro. Sure, his teaching abilities are outstanding, because he can explain concepts to you in many different ways. It is just challenging to listen to him without wanting to take a drooling kip in the middle of one of his lectures! So, if Amber would rather listen to *him*, she's really resenting this quest!

I slip from the chopper, the sun both warming and blinding. Squinting, I shield my eyes with a hand.

What time is it? I glance at my watch. It reads nine in the morning. I want to sleep until ten, even though I'd slept the whole trip, which just so happened to be through the night with Gali refueling at Brisbane International Airport.

To me this was a weekend or vacation. Both of which I usually sleep until around eleven. Well, on family vacations I'm awake at eight because Amber usually comes into my tent and jumps on my bedroll, and usually I'm too tired to care or start a blue. Most of the time, I just fall back to sleep as soon as she leaves. Then Dad will call me a bludger and tell me to join the living. That's usually when I drag myself from the tent to my family's cheering, and Mom slaps a plate of golden pickelets in front of me. The little pancake circles from the griddle are a cloud on my tongue. I start salivating at the thought of them. Yet, I believe those days of lazing around in my bedroll, and downing five and six pickelets are just a dream.

When my eyes adjust, I scan the scene. Everything has already been taken out of the cargo hold. A small river meanders before me, lazily burbling over and around rocks and logs. To the west, a small lake glitters in the rising sun, and mirrors a forest of Acacia and Eucalyptus trees. The same forest shades our camp, and some of the trees stretch their roots into the water. Shrubs of various kinds line the riverbank.

Somewhere in the bush a kookaburra laughs. Then a bird walks out onto the bank waving his white tail feathers about his face. A superb lyrebird. He's a beautiful bird, and a member of the peacock family. He struts about the bank courting. His sixteen-feathered tail resembles a lyre with the two outermost feathers making up the arms. Bands of black, browns and reds stripe these two arms. The inner, white, lace-like feathers form the strings. He chirps and sings his heart out, imitating all the sounds he hears, the whirring hum of the helicopter, a car alarm, and many other bird calls, most of which I do not recognize but sound mellifluous together. He repeats his kookaburra imitation. Then he walks back into brush.

"Holy dooley!" I exclaim. "It's no wonder we call that bird superb. That was amazing."

"They are very talented," Gali concurs. "I hate to run mates, but as you know, I need to close some distance between me and Adelaide. She shakes our hands then gives us a GPS. "We'll, be in touch. Keep this on your person so I know where to find you." Then she hops back into the Joey-242, and I watch her fly off.

Now it's just us. Two teenagers alone in the Never Never taking on a demon that is bent on destroying civilization, but from a secluded place. Cowardly. Why hide yourself from the people you are only going to wipe out in a matter of seconds. Surely, he has that power, or perhaps he doesn't and that is the reason he is hiding to conjure the strength to wipe us out. He'll never get the chance. We'll take him out before then. My overconfidence may be the end of me, but it does ease some of the anxiety that is slowly creeping up my spine.

"So..." Amber intones with a mouth full of egg salad sanger, "I reckon we should set up camp."

I shrug taking my own sandwich from my bag. "That's probably a good idea." I talk around egg salad, "You know, mark the dunnies and such." She jabs my arm. I stuff the last of the brekkie in my mouth.

"You might want these," suggests my sister tossing me my gauntlets. A grin of approval curls my lips as I lunge for the weapons. After composing myself, I turn on the GPS to see where we are. The little spinning circle appears on the screen, and then it shows twin lakes and a river flowing into one. The little blue triangle appears beside the words Koolivoo Waterhole. I look out at the lake. Lake Koolivoo. The name is probably indigenous or British. Most likely its indigenous since the founders of this country named most of the big smokes, Melbourne, Brisbane, Sydney after places back home. My curiosity quelled, I stuff the GPS into my pocket and walk several klicks into the bush.

Deep in the bush, I spot a young kangaroo and its mother. The two graze beside each other peacefully. The joey is at most a year old, but old enough to walk around outside of the pouch. The mother obviously has more meat on her, but to drag her back to camp, I would need another ten pounds of muscle, so the joey is the more practical animal to bag.

Some may classify my actions to be inhumane, but Amber and I must survive, too. That in mind, I take aim and let a knife fly at the baby. The mother scans the forest to see where the knife came from then abandons her baby. I walk over to the dying joey and relieve it from its agony.

Within a few klicks of the camp, distant cries resonate through the wood (they are the same yips we heard on our way to school). Thylacine. I pick up my pace to keep the gap between them and me reasonable. Judging by the numbers that were yelping, I guessed a pack of about six or eight strong. They must be tracking the scent of the joey slung over my shoulder.

The yelps of excitement draw near, so I break into a slow run. I reckon the dogs are about a kilometer or so behind me. That prediction ends up being fatally wrong, since one of the dogs, I assume the Alpha, leaps from the brush trying to drag the joey from my shoulders. My flight instincts kick in because hanging on to the joey is occupying all my fight instincts right now. I sprint from the pack, firing at the Alpha.

Amb's gonna kill me for this!

The camp comes into view, and Amber is lying on the shore listening to some tunes. I order her to make for the water, and my shout startles her. The music player flies into a bramble. She throws on her blades, as I drop the joey, and fire at the thylacines bounding for us.

The dogs glance at the joey, but just like those we ran from in Indooroopilly, these thylacines take a greater interest in us. Almost as if, some unforeseen force drives them. Why us, though? I begin to wonder if the demon knows of our presence, and sent these animals to take us out.

It doesn't matter, though. Just as Captain Cook battled sea and storm to reach the shores of Australia, it is going to take more than a couple of thylacine to stop the Hauksby twins from completing this quest!

In a triangular formation, they back us up to the water. I cast a glance at Amber. Frantically, she struggles to load her blades. Mine are already loaded. I hold my breath, aim and fire, only to watch the blades sail into the grass behind the pack. "Amb, you better have more luck!" I shout.

Finally, with gauntlet loaded, my fraternal twin takes aim at the Alpha. The blade pierces his flank and he retreats. The rest of the pack follow, taking the joey with them. We won, but lost our dinner that took me a while to find.

Then Amber backhands me across the head. "Good on-ya!" She says. "What is wrong with you, you boofhead? No, honestly. Did you think that bringing something that large back to camp would *not* attract animals?"

I have no rebuttal. Mostly because I knew that we couldn't have used that carcass after a few days anyway. We don't have any salt to cure it nor a place to store it, and I wouldn't want to contract food poisoning from a joey that's been sitting in a tree for a week. Even if we could stow the joey away somewhere, we are at least a thousand klicks from the nearest hospital, and out of range from any cell tower to call emergency personnel. That thought gave me pause. We need to be aware of everything around us. In essence, I wasn't thinking that through because my stomach was gurgling.

We make up, and she apologizes for the insult and for hitting me. I apologize for not thinking the way I usually do, which is ahead. I promise her from here on that small animals are on the menu. Whatever we don't eat, we agree to throw far into the bush.

"You know, I'll hold you to that promise even if it means throwing the whole kill into the lake." She would too, but when I make promises, I do everything in my power to keep them. Hopefully, she won't be throwing anything into the lake that I bring back.

We sit down on the bank eating granola bars.

My sister crunches on her bar for a few moments then says, "Okay Mike, here's what I want to know. Thylacines are extinct, right?"

"Supposedly, but there have been many sightings of the animal since it was officially claimed extinct in 1936, yet most of these have been hoaxes."

"I am aware of that Mike, but the animals we saw, both now and near Indro were clearly thylacine,"

I bite my tongue, afraid to admit a haunting truth. Perhaps, the Evil Spirit of the Shadow Flames resurrected thylacine fossils. He is a demon after all. Who knows what unearthly abilities, he possesses?

CHAPTER 4 A Cookout and Dilemma

MICHAEL

DINNER THIS EVENING IS ROTISSERIE white-winged fairywrens. I dump them in front of Amber.

The birds were a pain to catch, though one would not think so when looking at them: plump, blue pom-poms with an onyx bill (pointed and slender I might add) ideal for pecking at insects, black pearls for eyes and stubby wings that allow them to fly short distances. But those short distances were just out of my firing range. Then there is their tail. It seems disproportionately long for the rest of its body until the birds stand their full height, a little upwards of my ankle. It's also easy to distinguish the males from the females because the males have silver feathers surrounding their white wings, and they tend to stand tall or strut about like rats, while the females hop from male to male seeking a mate.

Guessing one wren was the equivalent to a tyke's half-portion of meat, I bring six. It took me most of the afternoon to catch them too. In the time it took me to retrieve our first meal,

49

Amber had set up our camp, tested the water for salinity, and gathered some kindling for a fire. She looks at the wrens, and then at me. Contempt contorts her face.

"What am I? A housewife from the 1800s?" she asks.

It had been her idea for me to do the hunting in the first place. I will never understand how the minds of teenage tabbies work (even if one of them is my twin sister). We may be twins, and sometimes we have similar thought processes, but she is a tabby and I am a bloke. If you spend any length of time with the opposite gender, you will quickly discover that women do *not* think like men, essentially speaking. Of course, there are exceptions to this rule. However, because we spend so much time together, some of the new schoolies think we're boyfriend and girlfriend who have mastered the art of keeping their relationship for after school hours.

Cooking the fairywrens qualifies as her share of the work because hunting doesn't take five minutes to accomplish as it does in the movies. That joey didn't just appear in front of me, you know, I had to walk through kilometers of bush to find it, and even then, you can't just raise your weapon and shoot, you have to aim. You have to make no sudden noises or movements. It's a lot of work to catch something. The fairywrens? Don't even get me started. I used at least six rounds on each of them, though I did manage to retrieve half the blades I fired.

My sister sighs reaching for her gauntlet blades, so I caution her about what she's doing. Amber examines the gauntlet in her hand and lightly fisticuffs herself in the forehead thrice.

"Come on, Amb. Use your noggin!" She says. Then she fishes through her bag for the hunting knife.

Again, I will never understand the mind of a teenage girl.

The avian flu virus already snared us after we spent a day on the beaches of Gold Coast. Catching it again is not an issue. We joked afterwards, and probably while we were sick, about how we'd wound up with it. Perhaps a gull coughed on us, or something to that extent. Sitting on the couch, we laughed at jokes we'd improvised, drank litres of tea, and downed bowls of homemade, onion soup. Let's not forget blowing our noses. Yeah, those were some good times!

I get busy gathering more firewood while Amber de-feathers the birds. Finding the kindling is the easy part, the challenge is finding a decent size log for the fire once it gets going. I have to walk a fair ways from the camp multiple times to gather enough materials to last through the night or at least until we hit the sack.

On one of my numerous trips to gather supplies, a wriggling worm under some forest roughage catches my attention. It's moving like a lure. Just walk away and don't look at it. If you don't look at it, you won't be tempted to investigate. No need to die of poisoning on your first day.

Upon my return, we both contribute to building the base. I place the twigs and grasses for the starters then Amber makes the tepee because every time I make one of them, it always ends up collapsing and smothering the fire. My sister's configuration, on the other hand, allows the fire to continue burning after the cone collapses. No matter how many times I watch her make them, I can never figure out her secret.

I notice the fairywrens ready to go on the fire, and they look tiny! But, in the fire, they go. I build a rotisserie rig out of two stable branches that are conveniently forked and narrow, yet also sturdy enough to support a spit, which I craft out of a branch filed to a point at one end with the hunting knife. (Basic survival tactics from our wilderness-exploring father.) I push two wrens onto the spit. My sister faces the other direction, and I ignite a piece of scrap paper I find in my bag. Gently, I stuff it onto the base, and we wait.

When I have the flames I want, I place the fairywrens over them. Amber turns to offer help, and the flames capture her attention. She stares into the fire, spellbound by the dancing flames. Absorbed with them, she rubs her scarred hand. The only other parts of her body that move are her eyes. I rotate the wrens and enlighten her about my encounter with the lure. She does not hear me, because the flames have her locked in a trance.

"Amb!" I clap my hands in her face.

"What?" She blinks and shakes her head. "Sorry, it's just every time I see fire I'm reminded of that night in our previous house."

"Yeah, it's hard to believe it's been almost a decade since that fire." I reminisce. "We were what? Four?"

"Six. And considering I almost lost my life in that fire, eight years isn't long enough. I'll admit I'm still terrified of fire. For years I've been trying to overcome it, but I just can't seem to shake that nightmare."

I start to cut-in, but she raises her index finger to say she's not finished. I roll my eyes. All right, I can wait. She rarely talks about what happened these days.

"Before you start judging me and telling me to just let it go, Le'me say this. You. Weren't. There. You did not see what I saw. You did not see smoke filling my room as the fire licked the doorframe. I never thought I'd make it out of my room. However, I had to try, so I kept low, but still coughed without rest. Had I not started screaming for help, I may not have made it."

"You do realize Mum would've pleaded with the firefighters to get you out of there."

"That's their job, yes. Yet, there is the occasional time where a firefighter will refuse to enter a house if the flames are too bad. They shouldn't refuse, since it is their job, but some make that choice. Sure, they try to enter the inferno, but I've seen the horror stories of a child trapped inside, the brave fire fighter running into the inferno to rescue them only to have the house collapse on both of them. Anyway, I made one last try to reach the window. After that, I don't remember anything."

I remember what happened during that rescue. Amber blacked-out at the window from smoke inhalation. Her hand caught fire. Thankfully, the firefighter smothered the flames before they could do any real damage to her hand. He hauled Amber through the window he'd shattered. When he brought my sister down the ladder, Mum showered him with gratitude.

Miraculously, the only burnt part of her body was her left hand. True, ambos rushed her to the hospital, but other than her hand, she was fine. The other miracle was that the smoke damage to her lungs was minimal, if any at all. Seeing her on that bed with her hand bandaged, and hooked up to a breathing apparatus that pumped oxygen into her body was heart wrenching for all of us.

When she finally awoke, and was able to breathe with just the apparatus in her nose, the firefighter came to visit Amber. He gave her a little, stuffed beagle (that she treasures to this day) saying that she was brave to crawl to the window to get help. The doctor's said she recovered quickly, and after eight years, you could hardly tell she had ever been in a fire.

But that night ignited the trauma she now endures. She suffered so much in the days that followed. We went camping that same year, and Amber refused to come near the fire. She sat at a distance and watched the stars. At the end of our camping trip, we visited family in Tasmania, and Dad asked Amber to stoke a fire. Amber argued with Dad until she cried.

At first, he thought she was being difficult, but then when the truth came out, he felt empathy for her, apologized and embraced her.

We've tried shrinks and everything, but I reckon it takes more than a few sessions to cure a near death experience. Her hand is a constant reminder of the night we almost lost her to faulty electrical work that Dad *swore* he'd fixed. I'd heard this story many a time too, but it never grew old.

I take her a distance from the flames before repeating myself. Using two fingers, I point to the general region where I'd seen the strange worm, carefully plotting my gestures so her eyes do not fall upon the flames again.

She cautions, "I reckon it's better if we just stay clear of that region then. The last thing I want is to be out here dying from an adder's venom."

I bob my head in agreement. Again, with no signal to call any emergency personnel for help, we want to avoid contact with anything fatal. We take note of the movement under the forest litter a few meters away. A worm-like tail wriggles about the ground. We freeze. The snake is too close to camp, so we have to do something about it.

Retrieving my gauntlet blades, I aim at the adder. I let a blade fly at the mound of litter. The tail ceases its luring movements as the sand and litter stain with blood. I cautiously walk in the direction of the tail and kick the mound. The snake looks dead, but I want to be certain. I grasp a stick, burn the tip and sear its belly. Amber looks away, holding her hand.

"Sorry about that, but you know me. Never leave things in the realm of uncertainty. Especially, if it involves a venomous snake."

"No worries. I understand what you were doing." She smiles at me.

We sit down away from the flames to eat. I do not want her looking at the fire while we need to discuss important matters. I bring up the problem of traveling to the Shadow Flames. First, we need to find them, so I glance around. The black crowns dance above the trees just to the south. So, we know where they are, now to discuss a means to reach them. Amber suggests a canoe to travel upriver. That would work except the river runs east to west.

"If you don't think a canoe will work, how about we head back to Indooroopilly and grab the Focus from the carport."

Amber must be joking! To walk one thousand kilometers, would be ridiculous. A month's worth of exercise. Sure, we'd see the heart of Oz, sleep under the stars, and be independent for once, but it just is not practical. We could do tasks that are more productive with our time than that. Not to mention we can't even apply for a license to drive, yet.

Then there is the obstacle about walking and driving through the Shadow Flames. We never actually walked through the wall, so for all we know, it could be a solid barrier or a viscous liquid, or even gaseous. It could also be all three. If I had to make a prediction, the wall is more than likely comprised of gases since we observed the shifting crowns of fire. We need to know what we are up against before proceeding. My sister agrees.

We have a starting point. Now, all we need is a means of reaching the Shadow Flames, other than walking if we can avoid doing so. Walking across the Outback is not exactly the smartest move by my standards, especially when almost everything in it can kill a person. We could find other means of transportation, though I see none presently.

Amber on the other hand, not willing to give in to defeat, takes a swig from her canteen and scans the forest. So keen is her determination that she does not notice her hand is a centimeter from a bird spider!

The spider rears up into its warning position.

"Amb watch your hand!" I warn.

She jerks.

The spider hisses, ready to strike at her. Neither of us have a phobia towards spiders, but I reckon, anyone would take precautions knowing these spiders possess venom potent enough to kill a human. Amber skewers the eight-legged crawly with her blade, and we hear a withering hiss as the spider's legs stand on end then droop. Amber cleans her knife on the grassy bank.

I'd read about the indigenous people of South America that used toxic covered darts to paralyze their kills. What if we do the same with this bird spider? I present the idea to my fraternal. She motions to the spider. It's hard to distinguish between guts and venom when everything is splattered across the limb. She turns around and starts scanning the forest, probably because of our original transportation dilemma.

I vedge-out against a tree. The Outback is relatively dead until nightfall since it's so arid, so I ask her what she is looking for.

She gives me a dumb-pan look. "Uh, Mike, it's winter. It's cooler now, so animals are more likely to be out during the day."

Fair enough, but I still believe she was wasting her time by searching the forest.

"If you have a better idea, you have my undivided attention, but sitting around," she gestures toward my slouch, "isn't going to do much is it?"

Despite her point, the only way I really see us moving is if a Land Rover drives by and we hitch a ride. We are not in the northern part of Queensland where water is more readily available. There is one rule in the arid parts of the Never Never: Carry lots of water or stay near a source that is not saturated with salt, which is rare.

A shape appears on the horizon. Amber faces me, a you-were-saying look on her face. My eyes shift skyward in annoyance.

You just love to prove me wrong, don't you, Amber?

The shape divides. I massage my eyes to make sure I'm not seeing double from lack of sleep. The shapes continue dividing. We struggle to make them out.

"They look like... wallabies?"

"Too large. Gotta be a troop of roos."

Amber turns to me with a glint in her eyes. My eyes widen as the thought shorts across my brain. "Hang on, you're thinking of riding a kangaroo across the Outback?"

A cheeky grin replaces her beaming expression. "You catch on quick."

I shake my head. Even if she does manage to wrangle one, a kangaroo is the furthest animal from a horse. The largest of Boomers (the males) do not have the body mass or the strength to support a teenage girl. He would simply collapse under her weight. Besides, roos are the champion kick boxers of Australia! Cheese them off, or frighten them and you'll probably walk away with a gut bruised for a week!

"Well, it looks like we're walking to the Shadow Flames then." She sighs. I can tell by the way she said it, she is not looking forward to hiking a hundred klicks or more south.

CHAPTER 5 The Scream From Hell

MICHAEL

PRECAUTIONS RISE AS LIGHT FADES. With clothes drenched from wading through the stream, we press south away from the sanctuary of our camp. Back in the city, I have no problem walking around after dark on lit streets, but out here is a different situation. I don't have a fear of the dark, I just need to be cognizant when I am kilometers from society and armed with the knowledge that a good number of these animals and plants are lethal. And yet, there is something different about this night.

When our parents take us camping the song of the night resounds like a mellifluous choir amid a whispering breeze, but in this brush as we walk toward the Shadow Flames, perfect silence shrieks the call of death, the evil to come. Each minute that crawls by, shadows swallow the last remnants of safety and our light. The encroaching darkness spurs my sense that something watches our every move. Waiting. Patiently waiting to spring out and slaughter us.

A rustling sound compels me to take a closer look, but caution trumps curiosity and I suppress the temptation. Instead, I quicken my pace to a slow jog, while Amber, confused about my sudden increase in speed, lopes alongside me.

"Why are we running?" she asks.

Without looking back, I point behind me in the general direction where the jostling thicket spurred my flight.

Amber suddenly bursts into a giggling fit, so I turn around to see her holding her knees and struggling to manage an apology. I soon take note of the reason for her hysteria. A frilled lizard scurries across the path and looks at us as it stands on the forest litter, his fan of skin stretched and his mouth wide. Her laughter is contagious, and I begin to chuckle too. I realize what I was running from is only as high as my shin. Laughing soon quietens, and she grills me with the one word question that often requires an essay to answer: "Why?"

"I dunno, maybe it's just the shadows of the night, or the fact that we're camping in the Outback alone, or we are hunting answers for something we know so little about. Despite the reason, I've been edgy since we started walking. Lately, I've just had this suspicion that we're being hunted. Or maybe it's just my imagination."

"It probably is just your mind running off on you Mike."

Why do I still feel peace is a carrot attached to a string that skips along the footpath ahead of me?

I flip open the compass. Good, we are still on course for the source of the Shadow Flames, I reckon. I hope. It would be frustrating if we walked all this way only to find we walked in the wrong direction, or the Shadow Flames suddenly took a different course to Brisbane.

I open my mouth to speak, but hold in the words. Amber stops walking, turning her head to me and waiting for me to say what I was going to say. When I shake my head, she shrugs and presses on. She and I can have an entire conversation without speaking a word. It's the beauty of being twins, I suppose. Although, perhaps that is true with a lot of siblings who are close.

Amber grasps my shoulder with the affection of a caring sister. She puts down her bag and suggests a little spar to relieve some of my tension. I turn the invitation down. A spar may release her tension, but not mine.

I want those answers to the composition of the Shadow Flames. Knowing at least that much, I may be able to sleep peacefully tonight. Since we began this quest, it was all I could think about. True, there is hunting, and preparing meals, but the Shadow Flames are always there in the background. Amber shrugs and shoulders her bag beckoning me to press on by taking off running through the brush. Not wanting to lose sight of her, I step up my pace until we run in stride.

My gaze lifts to the sky. Another day has come and gone. Stars barely light our way as we run south through the brush. Trees tower all around us, most of them growing in our pathway, so we slow to a walk.

I remove my bag and rummage through it for my torch. Amber shadows my actions, and we switch them on. The beams of light cast eerie shadows all around us. The forest is unearthly calm like the sea before the approach of a storm, a gentle whispering breeze only accentuates the ominous silence of the night.

The further we walk south, the quieter the wood becomes. It is as if the Shadow Flames swallowed up all life. Nevertheless, we continued walking. My beam arcs about in front of me as I load my gauntlets. If anything comes springing out of the brush to attack us, I'll kill it without hesitation.

Something grotesque and black, darts across the brush in front of us. I latch onto my sister and fire blindly into the darkness, missing my target. Amber breathes out slowly and elbows my stomach. Hard enough to make me let go, but not hard enough to cause injury.

"Relax Mike, it's an emu."

I squint to achieve a clearer view. The silhouette of a narrow head juts about as the bird walks. The head dips down and rises again. I illuminate the bird. It stares at us with an empty, dimwitted expression then bolts. False alarm. I breathe. Maybe I do need that spar more than I realized.

I drop my bag and torch at the base of a tree, remembering, of course, to turn off my torch, and stand in a back-L stance, which is a fight stance where one leg is behind the other pointing perpendicular to the foot facing the target. I also guard my face with my hands.

My sister eyeballs me a few seconds before she realizes my intentions. She sets her belongings next to mine, then we face each other and bow, and she takes a cat stance. It's like mine, only she places more weight on her back foot. It makes it easier to deliver a more powerful kick. She kicks first. I duck and knock her off her feet. Recovering rather slowly, she takes a closed stance this time. Everything is together. She guards her face and stands with feet shoulder width apart. I kick her in the knee knocking her down again.

"Av-a-go-yer-mug, Amb! Or are you purposely going easy on me? If the answer's is 'yes', then I refuse to continue sparring. Think of it as if you're actually sparring with Instructor Seung for our next belt."

Amber straightens up relaxed and unguarded. She brushes her hair behind an ear. "You initiated this spar remember? Whether we stop or proceed is your call. If you decide to call it off, I won't take a cheap shot at you. *However*, if you *really* want me to, quote 'av-a-go-yer-mug,' then I will be holding nothing back."

I ready myself in my previous stance.

"If you insist, but you were forewarned."

Amber leaps into the air, and just about nails me in the face. I block and grasp her foot. She twists out of my grip, and sends me headlong to the ground with the other. She offers me her hand to help me up. I refuse, and spring to my feet. She blocks my offense, and again I find myself on the ground. This is more what I expect from my sister. She lands every move, and keeps me at her mercy, while I am unable even to graze her. She lends me a hand. I take it, grinning. I use it to land a kick in her gut. (Just to clarify, the blows we exchange are not to injure each other.) A small victory.

We spar for a good ten minutes. As the sweat drains down my face, my stress flows out.

A whinny echoes through the night, disrupting the silence. I pat my face dry with my shirt, and I reckon Amber fetches a towel since I hear a twig snap underfoot. When I drop my shirt again, she tosses my torch. I reach to catch it. Turning it on, it flashes in the face of a wallaroo (a cousin of the kangaroo). I notice several others following it. Life had returned to the forest. However, the sudden reappearance of noise verged on peculiar and uncanny. They were loping north from the south, and judging by their erratic movements, I would say something spooked them. I lock eyes with a pair of yellow ones in the brush before us. A dingo leaps from the bushes. I shoot at it. It whimpers and collapses at our feet dying.

Amber demands to know my reason for just killing the animal. My answer is simple logic. Why risk becoming a wild dog's dinner? She claims my answer to be bull dust, and refuses to move until I make a proper rationale.

"Let me put it this way Amb. That dingo is replaceable. Dingoes give birth to around five pups a year. I can say with certainty the dingo population will not suffer extinction because in my eyes, I killed one in self-defense."

Amber covers her face with a hand shaking her head. "That dingo clearly had no intention of eating us. It was running from something just like those wallaroos were."

Clearly angered that I would slay an innocent animal, she removes her hair band and heaves it at me. I sidestep, and the hair band grazes my head. Then like a boomerang, it arcs around, sails through her hand and into the brush. She disappears into the thicket after it. Gloating that she missed I want to jeer, but she's already angry enough as it is. Doing so would only stir her pot further. Or perhaps not.

I know Amber is passionate about animals, though not up to an animal activist status, and she enjoys spending time with them. But is throwing her hair band at me really necessary? Once again, the mind of the teenage tabby is something that surpasses my understanding.

I look at my watch. Though only a few minutes have passed since my fraternal sister disappeared into the thicket, anxiety claws at my spine. Scanning the bramble with my torch for any signs of her, my heart rate quickens. Where is she? Surely, it doesn't take her this long to find a hair band.

My sister's scream rattles the night. I know it's Amber because it's at a piercing decibel, but following her scream is a sound that knots my innards. A belching roar that makes me think of Jurassic Park overpowers her piercing scream. I hear another sound, which I recognize as a thylacine yelping in pain. I pick up on the Doppler effect of twigs snapping underfoot. A few seconds later, Amber sprints at me, a look of horror pasted on her face, the hair band dangling about her neck, Her torch sways to and fro. She makes gestures, which I do not understand. As the gap between us closes she hollers to me, "Run, you dill!"

I scoop up our bags and run just as she bursts free from the thicket. As she passes me, she grabs my hand, and drags me through the woods. The trees blur out of focus as we charge through the brush.

"What are we running from?" I manage, through heaving breaths.

She doesn't answer. Silence reigns in the forest again. The only sounds I hear are my heart pounding and my sneakers beating the ground. Animals that hunt are silent. You never know they're upon you until they have you pinned to the ground, but by that time, they are usually attempting to spill your innards.

We keep generally to the same path we trod before taking a few detours and cutbacks to avoid the trees that stand in our way. As the trees blur around us, an animal waddles out in front of us. Seeing us approaching, the animal curls into a ball for defense. It's an echidna. (A relative of the hedgehog.) Amber and I bound over the prickly ball not decreasing our speed. I look over my shoulder. It would make my night if whatever hunts us would just bite into that prickly ball and get a mouthful of spines.

So concentrated are we on fleeing from whatever Amber saw, neither of us see the river come into view, and we run into it slowing our pace. Water soaks our clothes, and I realize we are upstream from camp, as Amber begins wading into the water. I dive and swim across.

Sanctuary at last! Our camp welcomes us home as it stands against the lake. On the edge of our camp, we drag ourselves up the bank and roll to face the sky, breathing heavily.

Gasping for breath, I huff a question, "What... exactly... did you... see... in there?"

Amber raises a finger and sits up clutching her legs as she struggles to regain normal breathing patterns. What astonished me was that she and I ran all this way within that short amount of time. Adrenaline can cause some supernatural feats. Amber draws in a deep breath. Dread is plastered all over her expression as she recalls the events of what she saw. It sounds too similar to a scene that might show up in a horror film.

While searching for her head band, she stumbled upon the Shadow Flames, (which had to be the only positive aspect to the whole tale). Overjoyed, she was returning to share the news with me when a low growl in the blackness caught her attention. She did what most people would do. She looked over her shoulder. A gleaming, serrated maw complimented the signature eyes of the Flames. She started to back away when it snapped at her. Then she ran just as a thylacine leapt into the clearing. Next, a giant lizard soon followed. From what she described, it was a goanna, which is a monitor lizard. The Shadow Flames continued to form them.

"Hold on a sec. The Shadow Flames formed them or they exited the Flames with the swirling around them?"

"It looked like they formed the animals, but I was too scared to analyze the situation." She smiles at me, and I know why. She has often said analyzing (even when I'm antsy about a situation) has always been my bowl of rice. What can I say? I enjoy knowledge.

I let her continue. She explained the two spotted each other, and then gave chase. The goanna leapt at the little dog a few feet from her as another thylacine emerged from the Flames and chased her.

"How large was that lizard?"

"As high as my waist. But he was occupied with the thylacine first, so I wasn't gonna stop and ask his intentions toward me."

A legion of the Shadow Flames attacking another legion. Well I reckon they are animals, so they'll do what animals do.

"The second thylacine that emerged overtook me within seconds of seeing me and snapped for my knee. Thank goodness, she missed. That's when I screamed and immediately pointed my gauntlet to her face. I impaled one of her eyes with a blade. She yowled in pain as she struggled to remove the blade from her wounded eye. I saw my chance to escape, so I took it."

Footfalls ring through the wood. Amber and I exchange fearful glances. I know I can run no further. She flops backwards on her knees sighing, while pulling on her weapons. To go another klick is a fantasy. Exhausted from sprinting, I wonder if we will even be able to face the lizard, or whatever it was that Amber saw.

I load gauntlets, and brace myself for the battle with Death.

CHAPTER 6 Amber's Hellborn Puppies

MICHAEL

WEAPONS RAISED, OUR THUMBS READY to launch the knives, we brace ourselves for what may be our first and last battle. I say first and last because our first two encounters with the Flames were not really battles. The first confrontation was with thylacines on the streets of Indooroopilly, and that time we were unarmed, so Maliu really fought that battle for us. The second time, they were interested in us, but ran off when we shot at them.

This time, however, would be different. This time we are going to war against a legion of the Shadow Flames. After this, if we survived this, there would be no turning back. We will be fully committed to completing this quest until we succeed or die in the attempt!

The sound of snapping twigs rises over the lapping waves of the river. I reckon Amber's thylacine has picked up our scent, and is running right for us, or it's a troop of wallabies again, I'm hoping it's the latter. Yet the marsupial is nowhere in sight. Then again, it is dark out so perhaps it isn't here yet, so I breathe relieving some of my tension.

Now that I think about it, part of me questions whether she imagined it all or actually saw it. Then again, it takes quite a lot to scare my sister. Amber switches on her torch, scanning our camp. Not a sound or sign of movement.

A beam of light makes a circular patch on the opposing side of the river scanning around the bank and shoreline the same way a searchlight rakes the sky atop movie theatres. The beam shakes slightly, giving the game away. Amber is just as scared as I am about this situation or more. Probably more because she saw the thylacine form, then it attacked her. Her torch falls on green shining eyes. The supposedly extinct marsupial shatters the brush landing with a soft thud before us. Its eyes shining in the light of her beam. The beast yawns showcasing his jagged maw, which opens almost one-hundred and eighty degrees. Closing his mouth, he stalks the bank, but that is all he does. He scratches and rolls onto his back, then I notice the pouch. She shifts *her* body, and whips to her huge paws. She continues to pace the bank. It's almost as if she is deliberately making herself our focus.

A twig snaps behind us. Amber and I whirl around in the nick of time to see three others emerge from the brush. I read in a book once that thylacines were ambush predators because their builds were not suited for running as dingoes are. The book also suggested this could have been a reason their numbers decreased as well, because they could not keep up with the dingo. It looks like the ambush portion of that information was accurate.

Keeping my arm steady, even though it vibrates like a guitar string, I let a blade fly. Amber fires a dual shot. We both miss the pack as our knives land somewhere in the thicket behind them. Searching for lost blades is like reaching into a Great White's mouth because the thylacines would be clawing and gnawing our backs. I decide that three lost blades are a small price considering our lives are at stake.

We load and fire again. This time my sister manages to pierce one in the head. A splash reaches my ears, and my neuro-net makes the connection. The thylacine we saw across the river is swimming over to aid her pack. Unlike the ones before us, she is no immediate threat, so I let her swim. I realize that decision will probably come back to bite me later.

I analyze the situation in nanoseconds. Amber said she fired an arrow into the eye of one of the thylacine, yet none of them appears to have signs of visual impairment. Perhaps the Shadow Flames possess an ability to heal anything birthed from them. To me, it is a logical conclusion, since the dog that attacked Amber the first time, now jumps at me fully formed. At the time, the others probably did not even exist. I point out my conclusion to Amber as one of the thylacine nips at me. I corral the nipping dog towards the others.

"Terrific, Mike! Now if you're finished analyzing the situation, could you help out?!" She fires another round.

"You're right. Sorry."

The pack surrounds us, and two of the beasts leap at me, while the other two challenge Amber. I roll, one of the dogs gaping jaws taking a gouging bite out of my side. Holding my ribs, I regain my footing. Shooting pain from the gash throbs rocking me on my toes. My sister somehow manages to take one thylacine out, so I follow her example to the best of my ability and trembling aim, and slay one myself.

In my joy, I forget about the other one, and he pounces on me. Pinned, I struggle to keep his maw from my face. The beast's jaws slip under my arm to close around my neck. In a panic, I slash at his face. The thylacine reels back.

Almost too fast to see, Amber whisks around and hacks at the hind legs drawing its attention away from me. Thankfully, I muster enough strength to aid my sister. Again, I slash at it drawing its attention back to me, and maim it. The thylacine leaps at me. It's momentum topples me into the river, and I see a blurred thylacine through a veil of water. The beast jumps into the water snapping at me. It would have finished me off had Amber not shot a knife into the monster's flank in mid lunge.

I drag myself up the bank. That tumble into the river leaves me dazed. The odds are in their favor, no longer two-on-two, but two-on-one. I can only pray that Amber will not share my fate.

I crawl further up the bank, breathing shallowly. The pain just about renders me unconscious, so I roll onto my back and lay still recovering. I'm out for the count. I do body inventory and find nothing broken, at least it doesn't feel as though anything is broken, so that's a relief. In the dim light, I take note of the wounds ripped in my side. Blood soaks my clothes, and I hear an electric pop. I know exactly what it is. The GPS fizzled out and along with it, our easy ticket home.

Using my jeans as a temporary bandage, I press them against the wounds. It helps quell the pain, but I still wish it would simply clot up so that I could aid my sister. Tonight there are casualties, and I pray we do not number in that count.

I feel horrible watching her battle those thylacines alone. I know it would muster all the strength I have left just to stand. She would probably hear me shuffling up the bank to help, and just tell me to sit this one out. So, here I lay, struggling to control my bleeding, and watching her battle it out with the resurrected beasts. The battle between the thylacines and Amber has me awestruck.

The thylacines pounce on her and maul her. I hear them shredding her clothing into what I can only assume is bloody rags. Yet, her screams are not of terror, but of determination, as she channels all her fear into a concentrated dose of adrenaline for strength, stamina and skill.

Amber stuns one by kicking it hard in the gut. Miraculously, she musters the strength to hurl the other over her head with her feet. Both recover quickly, and despite the gashes and nicks on her body, my fraternal sister staggers to her feet to face her foes with gauntlet blades pointing at each thylacine. They close in stalking low to the ground. The thylacines simultaneously leap at her, jaws agape in the infamous, near-vertical line. Amber waits for the last possible second, before she hits the dirt letting them collide. In their dazed state, she fatally stabs one.

Good on-ya, Amb! Show those thylacines you aren't playing around! That's three down and one to go, but my injuries shorten my breath, and my eyes grow heavy. I refuse to succumb to unconsciousness, not that I'm afraid of death, but for Amber's sake I desperately hang on to my wits.

The other notices me and bounces over to me. I brace myself to die. I know that seems cowardly, but it takes all the strength I have left to just keep my eyes open. Lifting my arm to defend myself may be the brave thing to do, but staying awake seems to be the only doable thing. Amber rushes past the one she stabbed, and draws the beast's attention by slashing its rump.

Ignoring her, the thylacine lowers its head ready to feast on me. In my peripheral vision, I see Amber walk away. Then she turns and rushes him hacking off its tail as she flies by. Our foe screams in pain and limps after her. Amber runs towards the river.

I summon strength from somewhere, and drag myself up the bank away from the battle. I collapse and turn my face to the battle. If this is it for me, I pray Amber will find a way to continue without me. Perhaps, she will find another ally to replace me. Yes, if I pass on before she finishes this battle, I will go to her in a dream and present my request to her. I'll request her to find an ally, so she doesn't have to do battle alone.

I turn my focus to the raging skirmish. The thylacine retreats up the bank after the first splash. There, it licks its wound. I know as long as I remain still, I will be safe.

"Awww. Does the wittle puppy not like salty water in his wounds?" Amber jeers.

The ancient dog cocks its head, looking at her, and then at me.

"Oh, no, you don't! C'mere!" She charges from the water, silvery blades glinting in the moonlight.

Bypassing the beast, Amber darts between it and me. I watch as the beast gathers strength for an attack lunge. It leaps. She waits for just the right moment to step to the side.

Amber extends an arm, the blades jutting from the gauntlet slice open its side. The hellish dog collapses with a yelping cry. A nauseating odor fills the air. The thylacine can barely move, as it lies dying. Amber seizes the moment and, using her blades on each wrist like scissors, severs its head.

Victory is ours, mostly hers, but we won!

My fraternal walks to the river and swishes the gauntlets in the saline water to rinse off the blood. She tosses her gauntlets to the dirt and kneels at my side.

"Amber," I wheeze, "you're game as Ned Kelly. What you did was incredible! If I don't make it... you must... continue without me. Australia... is counting on us to save humanity... even if the people do not know it."

Tears well up in her eyes. "Don't say that. You'll make it. You've got to. Please Mike, don't leave me, I can't do this alone!"

She jostles me, and I moan a little dazed. I've lost enough blood to black out at any time, so my sister acts quickly by tearing off her shirt, and ordering me to press it against the wound. She then runs to her bag returning with the first aid kit. She had wrapped her torso with a towel, and her own wounds stain it with blood. With a loose end of the towel, she dabs alcohol on my wounds. The remedy shoots a searing pain all over me, and I clench my teeth.

I must have zoned out for the rest of the dressing, because when I came to, Amber is slapping my face and asking me if I'm dead. She put a new shirt on me as well.

"Relax Amb, I'm just trying to sleep. No need to go bananas. All thanks to you, I'll make it through the night, I think." I reach up and squeeze her bare shoulder avoiding the slash wound there. "If you had not acted as swiftly as you did to defeat those monstrosities I may not have made it. For that, I'm in your debt. Now. If you don't mind. I'd like to recover."

She embraces me, and runs to set up my tent. After setting up everything, she attempts to carry me over. Despite my sister's wounds (and me weighing at least ten kilos more than she does) Amber manages to lift me and carry me to my tent. However, upon reaching my bedroll she staggers and just drops me into the open sleeping bag.

"Get some rest," I urge. "I'll be fine. Also," I pull the GPS from my pocket, "we're on our own."

Amber's face fills with fear, but then it softens. "We'll be fine without Gali. Try not to mull over it too much, all right?"

My face brightens with a smile as she hugs me again wishing me pleasant dreams and quick healing. Then she vacates my tent.

I hear the sound of her wading in the water. No doubt, she's rinsing her wounds. I hear the soft splash as she emerges, then the unzipping and zipping of her tent. The last words I hear before getting lost in my dreams is, "What a day."

I have to agree with her, for this day certainly has been awkward. These last few hours have indeed taken first place as the most frightening and challenging part of this quest so far, and we're bushed because of it. I have a sinking feeling that this is only the beginning of many gruelling ordeals. For now, however, shuteye is a blessing well deserved!

CHAPTER 7 The Whispering Eucalyptuses

AMBER

MY WATCH CHIMES at seven. Recharged, I rummage through my bag for a clean shirt. The sharp pain from the slashes across my chest brings the events of last night back into focus. Thank goodness, we had that first aid kit. I would have used my shirts as bandages if we hadn't packed it. I dress and vacate my tent. The crisp morning greets me, and I shiver slightly.

I breathe deep of the morning air. The rotting corpses foul the crisp air, and I wrinkle my nose. It reminds me of rotten eggs. Now, how to get rid of them? The lake? Duh. Then again, they might contaminate the water, so I better just leave 'em and cope with the sickening smell.

I busy myself to forget the smell, and what better way than to collect those knives we'd launched into the bush last night? I scan the brambles and tall grasses for anything glinting in the morning sun. Dropping to my hands and knees, I begin parting the grasses exposing the ground to sunlight. We hadn't really seen where the blades landed. For all I know some could be protruding from a tree.

Michael and I fired four blades in total, I recover two. Assuming the others are far enough back into the bush that looking for them could take hours, I decide to forget about them. After all, there are more important things to do than spend a morning searching for lost blades. I rinse my hands in the water; the shock of cold shoots through my arms, so I rub my hands for a few seconds.

After drying my hands on my Capris, I try carrying the corpses away from our camp. Each beast weighs about as much as I do. Even if I was at full strength, that much weight requires a second person, and Michael is out of commission for a while. That strategy isn't going to work. Perhaps, if I had some kind of axe, I could transport them in pieces. I go back on that thought remembering that I can barely stand the smell of them now.

Suddenly, voices hiss behind me. I strain to eavesdrop on their conversation as I collect twigs for a fire. I decipher some of the words.

"That's her. That's the girl who killed the thylacines last night."

"How can you be sure? She's kinda scrawny, and were there not two of them?" The other one murmurs.

"Yes. He's still sleeping. Besides, he didn't do much; she wound up killing the bulk of the pack. You were not there. I saw her use some sort of knife shooter to defeat them. How else do you explain the dead bodies?"

"I just find it difficult to believe, a gangly skirt like her can single-handedly take on four thylacine at once. We need at least one-on-one to pull off something like that."

"Believe what you want Des, but I'm going to inform Bastille and Zietas of this. You are welcome to join me if you desire."

"What about a perentie or a Komodo. You reckon she could take that on?"

"Doubtful. Come. Let's go."

I turn about to face the voices, and see two shadows retreating into the trees. I grab my gauntlet blades from my tent, and aim them at where I'd heard the sound. I fire a blade into the tree. Whoever they were, they vanished. The blades landed on the opposite side of the tree. I clean them off and place them back into my pouch.

Next order of business, play nurse for my recovering twin. I enter his tent. He smiles at me. "Happy birthday, Michael."

Michael stretches wishing me the same.

"How are you feeling?" I inquire.

"I'd say my scratches are healing quite well, nurse," he says.

A smile creases my lips. That's Michael, wearing his feelings like clothing. Last night, for example, when we were walking to the Shadow Flames, I knew just by the way he carried himself that something gnawed at his mind. Those suspicions were correct when he admitted he felt uneasy walking to the wall. Yes, I was bloody scared, too, but who wouldn't be? I'm the one who saw the ancient dog burst from the fires!

I examine Michael's wounds. Good. No sign of infection. I notice Michael has trouble pulling himself up, so I haul him to his feet. He stumbles out of the tent, tripping over the flap and we fall to the ground. Then we laugh. He sits up, grimacing from the pain of his injuries, and I can only speculate how his night must have been. Here he is, injured, in the Outback, hundreds of klicks from society. No way to rush to Emergency. No way to call triple zero for help. I'm grateful his wounds weren't fatal.

Michael glances over at me. "Aren't you, cold?"

"Actually, I'm rather warm," I reply. "Although, I am grateful we had the first aid kit with us. That certainly came in handy."

My brother hears my stomach gurgle. Brekkie calls, and since Michael is in no condition to do the hunting I take up the responsibility. He can be in charge of making fires. At least this way, I have an excuse to stay clear of the dancing flames.

The deal is set (though it really doesn't need to be). Michael admits he cannot walk around. If he *had* insisted on continuing with the hunting, I'd have ignored him and taken up the job regardless of the way he felt about it. After all, how hard can hunting be anyway?

I am so wrong! At nine I leave camp, and I wander around out here for hours. Michael could've returned with six meals in the time it was taking me to gather one.

Ironic how I despise the sight of fire, and yet I can make one in a minute. The temptation to return to camp and ask Michael how he returned with those wrens was in the back of my mind. Yet, learning by myself with minimal help from others is how I work. This strategy has benefited me to this day.

I pause. The same voices I'd heard at camp are here as well. Someone or some ones are following me. Whoever or whatever they are, their presence alerts a young kangaroo and it hops away. Remembering our pact to only bring small animals back, I ignore the loss. I walk around the glade calling up at the trees.

"Oy! It's no use hiding, I know you're there!"

No reply. More time for me to focus on my first task. After all, if I'm going to bring back anything to camp for brekkie, well, lunch now, I guess. That's where my attention needs to be , hunting. A galah perches on a branch just in front of me. Its pink head and breast sharply contrast with its grey wings. To kill such a beauty seems a shame, but I've come this far.

Taking aim, I let a blade fly. The knife hits the bird before it had time to fly off. Finally, a meal!

I'd marked my path with slashes to find my way back to camp easily. Michael is sitting against a tree napping when I walk in. He had put on a pair of jeans. The ruckus I make entering the camp rouses him.

"With all the noise you just made, I'm surprised you actually got that galah."

"For the record, that hullabaloo was to wake you up. Out there, I was quieter. It was weird though, voices in the trees scared off a joey that stood before me. I let it go remembering our agreement. This happened to be the next best thing so I , "

"Back up a sentence, you said you heard 'voices in the trees'? You sure you were not just hearing things?"

"Mike, have I ever lied to you?"

"You really want me to answer that?"

"Moving on," I swipe the air with a dismissive hand. "I've heard these voices, twice now actually. The first time they came from that tree." I point to the eucalyptus just behind his tent. His eyes follow my finger. But he is still not convinced. "I reckon there were two people, and get this, they were talking about me. One of them called me scrawny, and he seemed amazed that I took down those thylacines. The other doubted. Then they reported back to Bastille, who I reckon is the Evil Spirit Maliu talked about.

"Then, as I was out hunting I heard the voices again."

Michael points out what he *believes* to be the key flaw of my tale. He'd been awake all that time. He heard me target practicing on a tree, and pondering aloud what to do with the thylacine carcasses. According to him, I invented the story out of some delusional trauma regarding last night's events.

We decide to drop the topic and move onto our lunch. I prepare the fire and Michael lights it. While he roasts the meat, I decide to search for the other knives. At least it is better than uselessly staring at the flames reminiscing about my near death experience.

Something rustles the bushes beside me. My eyes dart toward the sound, and I set sights and gauntlet blade towards the bush. A shadow abandons his hiding place.

Somehow, I know he is scuttling back to Bastille. We can't have that because he could ruin our mission. He does not get very far. My knife strikes him in the back and he collapses. This isn't an innocent dingo. This little imp serves his evil leader. How do I know? Simple. He owned one of those voices, and the way he was sneaking away suggests his wormy intentions.

Walking over to him, I kick him and he half grunts half laughs manically. Well, it isn't the knives, but I have found a spy, most likely one of Bastille's thugs.

I drag him back to camp and dump him in front of my twin. Michael curiously pokes at him, asking me if this was my 'voices in the trees'. I haul the man into a sitting position by his forest green half-cloak. We study his attire.

He wears brown clothing, ideal camouflage for hiding in this forest. Calf-high boots cover his feet, and brass climbing studs, ideal for climbing, wrap both his soles and his hands. I pull off the hood. He looks malnourished. A young face, probably late teens or early twenties. Yet he has white-blonde hair, a sickly grey tinge to his skin, and grey eyes.

"Start talking." I interrogate. "Let's start with who you are and what you were doing in those bushes."

His face twists into an evil smile as he refuses to speak. I press my gauntlet against his gullet repeating my words. The man only continues to grin ear to ear. Perhaps he reckons my threat is empty, so I push with the blade until a trickle of blood seeps from his throat and still the mule refuses to talk.

His gaze shifts to Michael then back to me. "Listen, doll face," he finally says, very relaxed. "I serve my god, Centipede, and your petty interrogations cannot make me spill my guts."

Doll face? My eyes narrow. I pull the blade from his back forcefully. The man revels in my reaction. I kick him in the gut; he laughs and crawls away. I go limp. Thylacine and schoolboys are one thing, but forcing someone into telling me what I want to know is something I never seem to do effectively.

When he vanishes into the thicket, my brother explodes at me. "Why'd you let the man walk away like that? Why didn't you try different tactics to make him talk?"

I shrugged. "Michael, as you can see I have horrid interrogation skills. You saw his reaction to them."

Michael folds his arms as best he can, and looks accusingly at me.

"What was I supposed to do? Use Chinese water torture on him? I was holding a blade to his neck. I even pressed my blade against his throat! I drew blood! That should've made him at least spill something, should it not?"

The schmoozer said, "My fraternal, your method was too drastic to be considered a real threat. You should have just started by simply talking to the man or asking him questions that required only yes and no answers."

"The man refused to discuss anything with us!"

"You're not getting what I'm saying, Amb. To him, your tactics were bull dust." Michael says, shaking his head.

Come to think of it, *he* wasn't doing the interrogation, I was. "So I want to know how you might have done it since my method came across as a bluff."

Michael shrugged and sighed, "That wouldn't do anything, either. You saw the... whatever you want to call him. He had this look in his eyes that screamed he served something evil. With that I'm-not-telling-you-anything attitude of his, my way for getting people to talk could be just as useless as yours."

"Gee, thanks mate." I say.

"If you want something to take away from all this, don't jump to a knife next time, because most people assume it's usually a bluff."

Words to live by, although I have a feeling we've not seen the last of those. Ruefully, I look at Michael and say, "I'm going to call them Tree Leapers."

At around one, the two of us sit down to lunch. Not long after we do, Michael hears voices in the trees. He nudges me then motions for me to look up into the trees. Following his eyes, my eyes lock with the shadowed face of a Tree Leaper. He flees. Doubt does not cloud my mind. These are Bastille's dirties sent by him to keep us from investigating the Shadow Flames! I put on my gauntlet blades and scan the trees.

CHAPTER 8 Ground To a Halt

MICHAEL

USELESS. That is how I feel during this precursor to another fight, and only hours after our last one too! Shadows circle us in the canopy. I count off at least six. Amber refers to them as Tree Leapers. Though the name suits them, it is probably not their actual name. Nevertheless, regardless of what these tree jumping people are called, one thing remains in the realm of concrete fact. Their movements suggest they are taunting us. My fraternal tries in vain to follow their erratic branch hopping. I retrieve my gauntlets from atop my bag. Returning to my twin's side, I stand beside her, gauntlets pointing to the ground.

Amber launches a blade at random into the trees, attempting to hit at least one of them. No one falls. Nonetheless, we do draw them out of the trees. Six Tree Leapers land on all fours in a circular pattern surrounding us. One after the other stands in the order each landed.

They all have roughly the same physique: tall, and stick-like. As with the one we'd recently caught, each wears colors blending with the surrounding trees. The women wear skirts, and bikini tops. The men are clothed in trousers. Hoods shroud their faces. Each wields a weapon such as swords, daggers, bow-and-arrows, spiked boleadoras (those three-ball weapons that you throw to trip someone) and boomerangs edged with metal.

One battle scarred Tree Leaper stands out from the rest. Three furrows rake his torso. His black hair peeks out from his stained, mottled cloak. A metal gauntlet with four metal talons conceals what I can only imagine to be a horrific accident. I say talons because I only can count three fingers, and a thumb. Around his waist are two scimitars. From his waist down, he looks like the rest.

They have all the chips. A fight with them would only end with us dead.

Yet none of them engages us in combat. I feel surrounded by statues. What do they want? Amber glances in my direction. It takes effort, but I gather the strength to raise my gauntlets. I point one at a woman holding a boomerang and the other at a man with a bow-'n'-arrow. Amber guards another two, one wielding spiked boleadoras and the other holding daggers. All the projectiles are covered. That leaves the two swordsmen free. The Tree Leapers seem agitated. Tension peaks.

The one with the talons drops his hood. His jet black locks fall about his shoulders and tangle just above his empty, grey eyes. Using a talon, he brushes the bangs out of his face. His voice is smooth but conniving. "Must we have this conflict between us? I am inclined to simply talk about this matter."

"I say we just kill 'em and be done with it." A woman counters.

"Patience Hol. Patience. You'll get your chance in due time. For now, why don't we all just put down our weapons and sit in a nice little ring around that warm, cozy fire. Hmm?"

"Nobody asked for your smooth talk Zietas." Another woman cuts in. "Besides, we were given orders by Bastille to kill them."

"Cannot you see that we are in a circle, Ira?" Zietas says, running his talons through his lengths. "It just so happens to be the worst formation to fire projectiles, which three-quarters of us wield. Those of you who are willing to risk mutilating your fellow comrades to kill two tykes, can exercise that desire on a dingo or Joey. I'm certain either will give you greater satisfaction."

Some of them melt into the trees leaving three in our standoff. Another man, Ira and Zietas.

Zietas jumps straight to the reason why he and the others are here. "We want to know what you are doing here."

We fold our arms. Unless they give us the information we seek, neither Amber nor myself will spill. Tension rises again.

Zietas speaks. "Do you understand the seriousness of this little this meeting? This isn't some friendship circle discussing how you single-handedly managed to slay several vicious creatures with paring knives. You're walking a tightrope, because by having this conversation the three of us are breaking an order. Bastille is aware of your little spat with the thylacine, and wants you," he waved his hands dismissively, "eliminated. Tell us," he demanded. "How did you manage to slay those magnificent creatures? We will return saying the deed is done, and you two are free to go. However, you must abandon this mission."

Odious words. Amber and I stew. It's blackmail. In a way, Zietas told us he would be watching our every move to be certain Amber and I do not continue.

My twin raises her gauntlets to Zietas' face. I place my hand on her hand. She gives me a dirty look. Regardless of how she feels, now is not the time for heroics. Though I admire her courage to take a stand against this smug Tree Leaper, with me still unable to fight alongside her, it's three to one. Odds I feel will not end well.

With that, Zietas smiles and turns the floor over to the other man, who he introduces as Desoto. The man looks Amber up and down then at me. "Did this girl slay that pack of thylacines? How did she do it?"

He poses the question to me. Yet, Amber fought those monstrosities almost by herself. My gaze shifts to her for a response.

An exasperated, in-deep-thought expression wrinkles her face. Finally she says, "I just did what any person would do, defended myself. Happy?" She retorts.

"That is not what was told to me," Desoto replies quizzically. "I was told you kicked one, hurled one over your head with your legs, shot at one and hacked off another's head."

"I'm a little confused," says Amber.

If she's confused, I'm completely lost.

She has one of those attitude tilts to her chin, "If you already know how I killed them, what do you want to know?"

Desoto folds his arms. His reply surprises us. "I heard the tale, but I am skeptical of its truth. A teenage girl killing one thylacine is one thing, but one such as you..." his eyes rake her again. "I do not believe it." His expression holds no contempt, but is full of doubt. "A gangly teenage tabby should not have the physical capabilities to kill such a creature."

Desoto must not know about adrenaline. What shocks us is that he wants to see it with his own eyes. Solely, Amber is to face another thylacine in her wounded state! What he fails to realize is I had aided her for at least a quarter of that battle and killed one myself. True, she dealt the final blows, but the outcome may have been different had the two of us not been involved from the start. As expected, my fraternal refuses the battle.

Zietas points his scimitar at her. "You want to live do you not?" The lack of expression in his voice sends shudders through my body.

"What kind of a question is that? Of course I want to live!" Amber retorts.

"Then you will take on another thylacine."

Zietas provides no outs. Nevertheless, Amber tries her luck with requesting a rain check. Zietas laughs mockingly, because Amber's comment humours him. Ira stares blankly at us. Desoto on the other hand, entertains Amber's request. He inquires how long she would need to recover enough to face another thylacine, and Ira sides with him. A satisfied look brightens my sister's face. Yet, to me, the statement poses an equivocal meaning. I need to be certain Desoto's words are sincere.

"How does a week sound for you?" Ira inquires.

Amber hesitates. I can tell she wants more time, probably wanting simply to avoid the situation altogether. "Two weeks?"

"Eight days." Desoto barters.

"Nine?"

"Eight. That's it."

My sister blows at her bangs, while Desoto stretches then he urges Zietas and Ira to follow him with a gesture. Ira wishes Amber a quick recovery. Zietas requests to speak with Desoto out of earshot. We hear raspy whispers as the two undoubtedly discuss Desoto's agreement. I take note of their body language. Desoto droops. His attempt to delay before the fight may just have fallen through. Indeed, Amber may be facing another one of those hellish hounds.

The two turn back to us.

"Nah," says Zietas.

Zietas places a whistle in his mouth. Amber and I exchange nervous glances. She sucks in a deep breath. I pray she will not be killed in this battle.

"I tried to reason with him. Really, I did." Desoto says. Do I detect a faint expression of compassion in his eyes? Probably the sunlight.

He can feed that excuse to an emu. Amber looks just about ready to decapitate him, her anger boils that hard.

"You didn't try hard *enough*." She grits out between her clenched teeth.

"Actually, I was going to summon the beast, regardless." Zietas muses.

Another thylacine charges through the brambles. Amber shoots it in the eye and it cringes for barely a moment. The beast bounds towards her and leaps at her. Pointing her blades at the beast in defense, Amber bears the full weight of the speared animal as it crumples atop her. It whimpers in agony, falling limp. Everyone hears her struggling as she tosses the thylacine off her body.

The battle ended before it began. My sister brushes her hair behind an ear, smug satisfaction on her face. My jaw hangs open. Desoto and Ira are dumbstruck. Zietas slowly applauds my sister congratulating her victory.

"You do realize you defeated this creature in one-tenth of your previous time right?" I inform her.

"It had the same attack pattern, so I used what I knew would work." There is an edge of arrogance to her tone.

Zietas clears his throat, drawing our attention. "I expect you will be out of here within the hour since you won that little skirmish." He stands. Then Zietas clambers up a nearby tree and vanishes into the canopy.

"Oy, dipstick! We never agreed to that!" Amber hollers after him.

Zietas drops from the tree and walks over to my sister. "You agreed to it, knowingly or not when you replied: 'What kind of a question is that? Of course I want to live.' Unless," he runs his talons along his blade, "you've changed your mind?"

Amber glares at him, her cedar-red hair covers one eye. Zietas brushes it behind an ear and pats her face. "Keep sneering at me, you little ankle-biter, it will change nothing. If you like I can help you pack up your campsite, seeing as you are leaving?" We say nothing. "Very well, but you *will* be leaving within the hour." He vanishes into the trees.

Amber explodes when we can no longer hear the rustling of leaves. She refuses to move from the spot where she sits. Her anger toward Zietas clouds her judgement. Despite my suggestions to continue our investigations at home, nothing sways her. Nothing I say makes her move. She is a mussel in a pounding surf holding fast to its rocky home, a coral on the Reef.

I sigh and sit next to her. My chest burns as I put an arm around her. She blows at her bangs and hurls herself to her feet. Wincing, I grab her arm and force her down again. I want to discuss this matter, whether she agrees to or not.

"I reckon, you wanna talk?" She says. "All right, we were sent out here to foil the plans of a dorky demon who is trying to rid Australia of humanity. I'm not going to let some cloaked henchman of the enemy tell me to abandon this quest or die!"

"Amb, listen. I know you're frustrated, and you feel you've lost, but you haven't. You're alive! Zietas may have won this quibble, but that's all it is. When we're home, he cannot stop us from researching the Shadow Flames."

I know she heard what I said, but she walks down to the river. Then Amber disappears from my view.

Desoto returns within the hour to usher us home. Amber insists that she carry both knapsacks, even though she sports wounds from that first conflict, too. I can tell by her jerky motions she's still peeved by Zietas' blackmail, so I just let it go. Desoto takes us east, but only as far as Route 83 or Eyre Developmental

Road. There he wishes us luck and leaves us alone.

Amber allows her bag to slide off her shoulder. If my geography proves correct, we are roughly two thousand kilometers from home. No matter how we slice the pie, the trip will take, at the bare minimum, ten days on foot. We'd take the first sign of transportation, but for now, we are walking. The best course of action is to follow the roads.

I decide to head north on Route 83. Then Amber turns south. She glances around and begins her trek toward the Shadow Flames.

"Where're you going?" I call after her.

Amber stops mid-step, still facing south. "You're smart, figure it out."

If I know Amber, she is researching the Shadow Flames until Zietas forgets about her. What she may not realize, or perhaps does and just doesn't care, is that we're on his turf. He can track us. It's a mistake she'll regret if I don't act, so I hobble after her.

"If you're coming to tell me the risk involved in going to the Shadow Flames, I already know what that entails. Just so we're on the same page, I don't care about the risk.

We came out here to destroy these Shadow Flames, and that's what I intend to do. No tree-leaping dipstick is going to tell me otherwise." Amber faces me. "Got it?"

Loud and clear, sis. "Amb, be reasonable, if you die, your cause will be for naught."

"No, if I sit on my arse and do nothing, my cause will be for naught."

Never try to change a headstrong tabby's mind. Trust me, mate, it's not worth your time. So following my own advice, I hobble after my fraternal sister as she walks south.

CHAPTER 9 Doppelgangers Born of Fire

AMBER

HEADING SOUTH toward the Shadow Flames is more nerve-wracking than swimming off the Gold Coast with a shark watch in effect. Every step I take toward the Shadow Flames, I feel a swelling presence of evil. I mean, I know the Shadow Flames are evil, but this is something more. It is almost as if I can sense Bastille's presence. It could be Uli's blood that makes me sense this. I'm not sure. Maybe I'm antsy about another thylacine rushing from the flames and mauling me. You never forget something like that. I mean, it's one thing to see the dog, but having one pounce on you with fanged jaws gapping, that's a whole higher level of creepy!

A hand grips my shoulder. It's Michael's. He wheezes trying to catch his breath, so I stop, giving him a break.

"You want me to carry you?" I offer, tapping a foot.

We've had to stop several times already and my patience is wearing. Sure, I'm amazed he's holding up, but at this rate, we'll reach the

Shadow Flames by two in the morning. A set back, I would love avoiding.

He asks, "How much do you weigh?"

I manage a grin. "Mike, word of advice, never ask a tabby that question. It usually doesn't go over well, but since you're my twin, I weigh fifty-two kilos. And before you start calculating whether or not I *can* carry you, I'm going to carry you anyway, so get on."

"You really have to stop reading my mind," he says. "It's really weird," I'm his twin. We think alike, and as I've said before, he wears his emotions. "Besides, you're already carrying the two bags, how do you expect to carry them and me?"

I would find a way. Sure, I may struggle for a few minutes, but I would discover a solution. Then again, the minutes I spend bumbling around with sixty-some-odd kilos on my back, I could be walking.

Michael stands. "Shall we?"

"Can you, because we can set up camp if you wanna call it a day."

I know I said before, I wanted to press on, but my brother's wellbeing means more to me than reaching the Shadow Flames today. If he wants to call it a day, I will oblige.

"Nah, I'll tough it out."

I shrug, and we press on.

We reach the Shadow Flames as the sun bathes the Outback in an orange glow. The wall of fire rumbles and crackles before us, but it feels cold. I rub my arms as a draft blows strands of hair across my face. I look up the wall of fire to the tips licking the heavens. I cringe. Why does it have to be fire? Of all the things it could be, why fire?

Michael reaches out to touch the flames, and I slap his hand scolding him. Usually, I don't play the analytical one (that's Michael's expertise) but this time I'll make the exception. We don't know what these flames are, for all we know they could be one of those vacuum like voids you see in science fiction films. You know the kind of void that sucks you in when you get too close. If my twin wants to probe the flames, he can use a stick or something.

Then a perentie lumbers out from behind a rock. It waddles across the ground at our feet. The perentie is the largest lizard native to Australia and the ankle-biting cousin of the

Komodo dragon. We watch it walk into the flames.

The flames roll back like ocean waves ebbing from shore. The line, where the flames once stood, snakes at our feet. The flames swirl enticingly, but I take a few steps away from the fire (pulling my curious twin by the hand with me, I might add).

Suddenly, the Shadow Flames swell and roar past the line. Michael leaps back nearly taking my arms off. Then as they settle, the perentie bounds onto the plain, standing at our knees.

"Mike... what happened to the perentie?"

"I think that's it? But it is the size of a kamodo."

"It is a kamodo," I swallow.

I turn to run, but Michael grabs my shoulder. "Don't run, he'll give chase and overtake you."

"So what am I supposed to do, stand here?" Then I say, "Just use your noggin, Amb! You have a weapon." I fire a double round at the lizard's eyes. The Komodo charges me. Michael pushes me out of its reach, and instead of me, the Komodo clamps around his ankle.

Before I can stop it, it drags my brother into shadows. The fires retract again. I don't want to lose my brother, but I freeze. A shadow Komodo, just pulled my brother into the fire. What other unspeakable horror could lurk within that black veil?

The fires begin to entice me again. This seems familiar. Next thing I know it will be my brother's shadow emerging from this fire. I swallow. It's fire, and fire terrifies me, but Michael just saved my life, so to let him become the next victim of the Shadow Flames is well, he'd have done it for naught. Closing my eyes, I breathe deep then sprint into the flames.

Antarctica wraps icy arms around me the instant I run into the flames. Immediately, I stop running and rub my arms, shivering. And though I've never been to the bottom of the world, I'm sure this cold compares to a warm day there. On top of that, the darkness surrounding me is complete. I cannot see my gauntlets when I place them right in front of my face. I grope about in the darkness and trip over a bush then a rock, and then I walk into a tree. I do it again.

Great I'm running in circles.

I switch on my torch and point it at the ground. The dirt, like most of the Outback is red, and the shrubs are yellows, and olive greens. I see the Acacia tree that nailed me twice in the face, or at least I think it's the same one. It's hard to tell unless I left visible markings on it, which I don't see, so it's probably a different one. For all I know these flames could stretch several klicks before me. Either that, or I'm still walking in circles.

No, I'm definitely walking forward because my beam is pointing forward. My torch illuminates some of my surroundings. I'm not walking in circles anymore. A plus. I can see. Using it, I search about to find my brother.

"Michael!" I holler into the blackness, shivering. My beam arcs from side to side. No reply. All I hear is the Flames' drum roll and a whistling wind. I try again.

Then the light goes out, and with it my hope of finding my brother. Footfalls reach my ears. A white light flails widely towards me, behind it two green lights.

Then the light disappears, but before me two green eyes dance around.

"Your brother belongs to us now, Amber." A raspy voice echoes through the blackness. "Had you acted quicker you may have been able to save him."

"Yes, she may have, but I doubt it. The Komodo's saliva will be the end of him." Another voice jeers.

Both laugh.

I slash at the blackness. A shriek splits my ears, so I must have hit one of them, whatever they are. Then a hand reaches for me from behind, and it's my turn to scream. A hand covers my mouth, so I bite down.

Michael yelps in pain, cursing.

"You shouldn't sneak up on me after I just heard two people tell me you were just dying at the saliva of the Komodo."

"What? I'm right here, Amber. How could I be taken and be dying if I'm right behind you?"

I turn around. Michael shines the torch in his face, smiling. He flicks his head.

"C'mon Amber, this place is cold and creepy, let's get out of it."

I follow him.

Suddenly, I stop. I ran into the flames from behind me, so why then, are we heading further into the flames? I ask Michael to give me a break. He pauses, but shines the torch in my face. I squint and hold a hand to shield my eyes. Michael doesn't take the hint to remove the torch.

"Mike cut it out will ya?" I ask, but there is still no compliance at his end. "Michael you've had your fun now stop shining the torch in my eyes."

"Are you ready to press on?" He finally asks.

What? Where did that come from?

Up until now, I've believed I was following my brother. There is something different about him. I can see him toying with me like this for a little while, but now this game is starting to aggravate me.

"So, Ballerina, are you ready to press on?"

I shake my head in confusion. Hold the phone, *Ballerina?* That was his nickname for me when we first started Taekwondo. That was when my kicking was up instead of out. He stopped calling me that last year. Why was he saying it now?

You know that little voice in your head that tells you to get out of a situation before it gets worse. I've been hearing that voice for the past ten minutes or so, and ignoring it. Only now do I clue in.

Amber, what are you doing? Turn and flee from this evil place! Who you see before you is not your brother.

Okay, I'll bite. If it isn't my brother before me, then could it be a figment of my imagination?

This is no apparition, but the evil power of the demon. Inquire about something you know Michael would not know, and see if this Michael does know the answer to that question. That should lay to rest your doubts.

I need to think about that. What does Michael not know, that I don't know either.

Ask if the demon is taking the form of a man or a woman, the voice suggests.

The question sends my head spinning. Why gender? Do demons even have genders? Then there is the voice. It is not mine, and it's certainly not Michael's, so whose is it? For that matter, how does it know my name? Still, the question is better than anything I can conjure up, and since I don't know the answer, Michael may or may not know it.

"Hey Mike, Bastille is a man, correct?"

"Don't be silly, Amber, you know Her Majesty is a woman."

Bingo. Thank-you Michael's Shadow for proving to me, you are not my brother. My doubts lift, the voice in my head fades with the doubts, but I don't mind. I have the information, so I smile at my twin's doppelganger. It must have seen my expression change, because I suddenly cannot see anything. Then a perpetual shriek splits my ears. I fall to my knees, cupping my hands over my ears. The voice returns to my head.

Amber, get to your feet, and run. Run from this place!

What have I got to lose? I jerk to my feet still cupping my ears, and run. My heart pounds. My legs burn, but I run. My breath wheezes, my head feels light, but I keep up my pace. Michael appears in front of me, so I slide to the ground and make a billowing cloud of sand splatter into his face.

Michael doesn't move. "Why are you leaving me, Amber?"

I frown and push past the doppelganger and continue running. A white ball of light abruptly appears and races ahead of me.

Follow the light, Amber.

So I do. You can say I've gone round the bend, but this voice did just tell me I wasn't following my brother, so I listen to it.

My foot catches the root of a tree, and the ground races toward me while blinding light floods my eyes. Then I realize I'm no longer in the blackness of the Shadows Flames, but staring at a patch of grass in the Outback. I get up and brush myself off then glance around.

"Michael! Oy, Mike! You out here, mate?" No reply. I'm alone. It is as the shadows said. If I had acted faster, I may have been able to save him. No, they are wrong. I still can save him, as soon as I figure out where I am. But where exactly am I? The surroundings do not look familiar.

There are no street signs, no Indooroopilly Shopping Centre to point me in the right direction. There's just Outback in every direction. An open sandy plain from which grasses and a few acacia trees sprout. Exhaling, I feel a tug to head west. I don't know why, but

I do. Maybe it was the source of the flames; maybe I was closer than I thought I was. This quest will be over soon and I can get back to my normal life!

But something tells me after this, my life *won't* be the same as it was. I'll be different. I'll have a story. Likely, many will think I have kangaroos loose in the top paddock when I tell them.

What am I saying? Who cares what they reckon! I know I did it, and if they choose not believe me then that is their choice.

Suddenly, a black sickle rips a wound in my shoulder. I whirl around, pointing gauntlets at the Shadow Flames. Michael's doppelganger emerges from the fire, my blood dripping from his sickle-blade-hands. Ghostly green eyes radiate evil. The doppelganger stands my twin's height, and his bleach wisps vaguely resemble Michael's hairstyle, but the rest of his body is a silhouette. He has a mouth, but it lacks teeth. His face is void of most features; however, I can make out a nose. He wears baggy trousers and parades topless, displaying a toned upper body, my brother's body.

Another one steps from the flames. Come on! Really? I have to face both Michael and this evil clone of me? Could this day get any worse?

My doppelganger's hair is a raging mane of white fire, and slightly longer than mine. The fire hair coalesces into wispy red strands mimicking fire. She also has sickles for hands. Her lips curl into a toothless smirk on a face void of features, and she wears an ankle length robe that reminds me of the grim reaper. From what I can see, her body is identical to mine: Same height; same feet; same boney ankles and wrists.

The only part of their bodies that remain fire is a rapidly spiralling 'X' on the stomach. Both spin clockwise, but Michael's is closer to his chest. My evil's 'X' appears to be as much part of the robe as it is a part of her body. The vortex rotation spellbinds me. The fire swirls like a perpetual whirlpool around a white center. It's beautiful and eerie, sort of like a whirlpool in the ocean. My clone seizes the opportunity to charge me, managing to knick my side.

"Give up, while you still have life in you," taunts my clone, but The Voice tells me to stand my ground.

I was going to anyway. I raise my blades pointing one gauntlet at each doppelganger.

"You never did know when to admit defeat Amber!" Michael's evil says, rushing me.

I let a blade fly.

CHAPTER 10 Shadow Strike, Lost Cause

AMBER

WHAT? I MISSED? How could I miss? Shadow-Michael was rushing right for me, and I missed? Still, not wanting to be run down, I retreat facing my opposition.

Reloading and firing another blade, at my double, I aim for the vortex, because that's where you would shoot first, right? Unstable, not completely formed, you know the usual thoughts that come to your mind when you see something like that.

The blade impales her, but she doesn't wince. A storm rages in my head as I make the aggravating connection. I didn't miss Shadow-Michael, I just wasted a round on him because it passed right through him! Shadow-Michael stops and chortles, while my Shadow folds her arms in satisfaction.

"We tried telling you Amber, but like I said, you never know when to accept defeat. I'll admit, watching you try vainly to graze us was amusing, but I'm afraid we have to do away with you now."

Both he and my shadow rush me. I ready myself, hoping there may be a chance of grazing them. Then that voice returns to my head. It tells me to cast the shadows back into the fires.

"How?"

… Seek and you shall find, knock and the door will be opened to you…

Those words don't help me right now! Knock on a door? What door? The only thing before me that may pass as a door is the Shadow Flames, which is probably not what this Voice means. Seek and you shall find…? Seek what? The Voice? Might as well try it.

The dopplegangers lunge for me, so I dive to the ground. My double sees me and contorts her body to make another blow at my arm.

Since when was I that flexible? Oh right, I'm not. But she is because she's my evil clone, and she's born of the Shadow Flames, so she can do more than me.

The pain stings, and I look up to see her lick my blood off her sickle. All right, that's gross! Then I remember the words that voice told me. *Seek and you shall find.*

Any time now would be great, whoever you are?

Suddenly an arrow impales Shadow-Michael in the eye, and he moans in agony. Right on! Whoever you are. Shortly after, another pierces Shadow-Amber. The two of them struggle to remove the arrow, but sickle hands manage to slice it in two. Shadow-Amber tries to pull it out with her wrists.

Call me sadistic, but their pain is satisfying. I make doubly sure they're still occupied with removing the arrows then I reel my head around wondering who fired the arrow. All I see is the empty plain of the Outback. I turn back to face my foes, but the last remnants of them swirl with the sand on a breeze.

Amber, now that you are safe from harm, I want you to make for Simpsons Gap in the MacDonnell Ranges. There you will find the means to rescue your brother from the Fire.

Forget that, I'm going to free my brother now, finish this quest and go home!

It is written, "Whoever is patient has great understanding, but one who is quick-tempered displays folly." Amber, if you rush to face Bastille now, you will not succeed. In time you will rescue your brother."

Says you. Besides, for all I know this could just be one of Bastille's tricks to see if I'll walk out. Sorry Bassie, but this girl's gonna rescue her brother and you can't stop her!

Midnight comes and passes, as I take a rest on the ground. Michael's true birthday. Yesterday, I turned fifteen, today Michael does. He was born five minutes after me, but it ended up being a minute passed midnight. We celebrate it as a family, alternating it each year. This year we would have celebrated it on my day. A tear trickles from my eye, and I wipe it off my cheek. Michael's face flashes before me in the sky. I see his spacer, his schmoozing smile, his laughing eyes.

An ache comes over me as I realize I would give anything to lie here with him reminiscing about our past birthdays, and the fun we had at them. To be at his side again, to listen to his theories and analysis of what he found out about the Shadow Flames while in them, to hear how he escaped that Komodo in his injured state.

"Happy birthday, Mike," I say, my eyes filling with tears. The river of tears overflows down my cheeks. I don't try to hinder it, because I need this cry. Bastille took my brother away from me as a birthday present, and she'll pay for it with her life! For now, though, I'll let her live another day, since I'm three hours west of her, and sleep beckons me to lay down my head.

A sense of despair creeps up my spine. I was sure by now I'd have some clue as to where he is. A sign. Something. Anything. Anything he would've thrown out of the fires to say I was on the right path, but all I've seen is Shadow Flames and Outback. Oh, what I'd give to see anything that points me in the right direction!

Suddenly, a thought occurs. I could have missed the sign. It is midnight after all. That had to be it. I missed his sign, he did throw something out of the flames, and I kicked it under a bush or something. However, to go back and search for it would take too much time. I ignore the voice. What's in Simpson's Gap that can help me? I press on following the Shadow Flames westward because to know you enemy you have to study your enemy. Besides, I know to the east is Brisbane.

A yawn rises in my throat, as I stretch. It's been a long and grueling night, but I need to press on. Groggy, I stand and continue westward. Hang on Mike; just hang on a few more hours. My feet give out and the ground rises toward me, and everything fades to black.

I awake to a kangaroo's nose wallowing in my face. He begins licking it, and I giggle pushing his snout away, but the boomer persists, so I reckon there's something on my face he enjoys. I sit up, forgetting his face is right above mine, and we both sit dazed for a few seconds. Then, he grows bored of me, and hops back over to his troop. I watch them from where I sit. Three stand guard while the others graze. I reach to wake up Michael, but then I remember he is in Bastille's clutches, or... No, I don't want to think that. Shadow-Mike and Amber are wrong!

The events of last night come rushing back to me. Michael taking the fall for me, the confrontation with his shadow, and me believing I was actually talking to my twin!

Amber you dill! How could you mistake a copy for your own twin? He walked ahead of you, not beside you. He didn't talk once to you. How could you? I let out a groan of frustration, and tug at my hair. I press fists against my face.

"How could I mistake a doppelganger for my twin?! The thought of it is just... just... uhhh! Amber, you egghead! He's your twin, your blood." By now, I'm pacing the Outback. "You're other half and you, " I stand stil from a moment and breathe deeply trying to compose myself. "You made a mistake. Everyone does. Just let it go, and move on. You'll get him back, and when you do, you'll tell him this and we'll laugh about it. Just deep breaths." I draw in a breath and hold it for eight seconds (apparently that is what you're supposed to do when you're stressed out), and I let it out. "Deep breaths. That's it, just breathe and forget about it. Breathe in..." I draw in. "And out." I exhale. "In... and out. In... and out. Now forgive yourself."

I feel better. I probably just needed to get that out.

The kangaroos move on, a reminder that I should, too, but my stomach gurgles as I stand. Right, I missed dinner and now I need brekkie, but being miles from the bush, and with the troop bounding away, what is there to eat? I rummage through my gear, and my fingers wrap around a crinkling wrapper, encasing a bumpy, rectangular bar, so I pull it out, a grin crossing my face. Well, a granola bar is better than going hungry. I struggle with the packaging. It is last minute breakfast proof. How does one get this off? Finally, after a good minute of trying everything from using my teeth to stepping on it, I resort to cutting the bar in half with the army knife. Then, I savour the nutty, honey-smothered-goodness. And then... it's gone. On the bright side, I have enough energy to find a proper morning meal, or if I'm lucky, Michael. That way I won't have to make a fire, and sit before it fearing the flames.

I stand, stretch, and continue my course westward.

A klick from my makeshift camp, the feeling of someone shadowing me has me on edge. Turning around I scan the plain. There are a few decent places to hide, a bramble here and there, a tiny outcrop of rocks. But the plain is barren.

Surprise! When turning around my nose grazes the tip of a scimitar. Then surprise boils into annoyance as I follow the blade to a metal, four-fingered hand. Zietas. My eyes meet with a grinning, shrouded face, but he doesn't remove his hood. On his cheek, I notice a smear of crusted blood. Good-on-ya Mike! My spirits lift. This is the sign I've been waiting for. Zietas will tell me where Michael is.

"You wouldn't happen to be breaking your promise to abandon this quest and go home, would you? Because if you are, I will not think twice to run this sword into your gullet." Zietas says.

I swallow, looking at the tip of his scimitar, "I'm, uh, rescuing my brother."

"So you are admitting to going back on your word then?" Zietas removes the sword from my throat. "Though you didn't say it, you did tell me, because your actions caused your brother to end up where he is, which by the way, was a brave act on his part. He didn't have to do it. Since he did take the fall for you that means you never actually went home in the first place. Don't try to tell me otherwise, for you will only be lying to me. Now Amber, your brother suffers from your mistake. So tell me, my dear girl, is that fair, having him take the fall for your arrogance?"

I glower at Zietas, pointing my gauntlets at him. "My brother is where he is because a

Komodo dragon toyed with us, and dragged Michael into the flames. It had nothing to do with me. Besides, he wanted to complete this quest as much as I did. I intend to rescue my brother even if that means taking you and Bastille out!"

"Your confidence is amusing Amber, I'll give you that, but I'm afraid, it will not save you or your brother." Something in his tone I did not like.

I fire a round at his face. Zietas contorts his torso leaning vertically, and the blade soars into the sand behind him.

Then he rushes me ripping a wound in my side. I bite my lip, struggling to contain a scream as a tear trickles from my eyes. Through blurred vision, I see his foot nail me in the same wound. Next thing I know, my hair is in my face and I've swallowed a mouthful of sand. I struggle to regain my footing, but Zietas kicks me again, this time in the ribs. The kick lands me on my back where I'm pinned under his foot. He presses the tip of his scimitar against my cheek and flicks his wrist.

You know when you cut yourself with a knife and there's that short window of time, where you feel nothing before the sting? Same here. By now tears stream down my face, and blood trickles from my wounds pooling at my side.

"You know Amber, I would have thought you'd have put up more of a fight, but I guess a thylacine is your limit."

His hand reaches for me, and it takes all the strength I have left in me to slash at it. A drop of red falls on my forehead, while Zietas reels back sucking his finger. He reaches again for me this time my feet, so I kick him, but I only manage to give him my ankle. He uses that to hoist me into the air. My shirt falls into my face, and though I can't see, I still thrash hoping to hit him, but the pain of my wound hinders my movements. Zietas throws me to the ground again. Then he slings me, dazed and bleeding, over his shoulder. I've lost. Michael, I'm sorry, I failed you. I should have listened to the voice and headed for Simpsons Gap. Had I done that, maybe Zietas would have never found me.

Suddenly Zietas grunts and drops me, and I stare at the bare foot of an aborigine, as darkness clouds my eyes.

Book 2

Mind tricks cloud and burden.
Death laughs at our struggle,
But Light is peace
Where self is put to rest.

CHAPTER 1 The Eye Of Retribution

MICHAEL

A few hours before Amber's struggle with Zietas.

CAVERNS, THE SOLE WONDER OF NATURE that terrifies me, and Bastille's domain rests in the heart of one. The ridiculous aspect of my fear is that it's self-inflicted. During a trip to Capricorn Caverns, I strayed from the group and crawled into the Rebirthing Tunnel, a narrow, rocky shaft in the side of a wall. I clambered through wrong, I reckon, and got stuck. Then I had to sit there for five minutes before someone pulled me out. I've been afraid of caverns since.

The thought that turns my wheels is how I wound up here. I must have blacked out when I saved Amber from the Komodo because I have no recollection of the events following that. I sit up, pressing my palm against the damp ground. Alert, I raise my hands to my face. Skin touches skin. Ace! Those dastardly thugs removed my gauntlets while I was out! I purse my lips, and tap a finger against my hand impatiently.

Swift footsteps plod toward me somewhere down the tunnel. I try to crawl into the shadows of the tunnel. A lanky, emaciated woman struts into my view. She wears a robe with drooping sleeves and hooded cloak overtop a simple tiara. Her eyes are emerald green, her lips, the color of charcoal, and though her face is haggard, youthful features peek through. Her eyes scan the tunnel and fall on me. I freeze as wonder floods her face.

"And who might you be?" She asks, walking to me and stooping to my level as though I'm a child. She extends a hand craggy with wrinkles. Then again, seeing as I'm cowering in a corner, I see how she could see me as a child. "Well, come on, I won't bite."

I stand. "The name's Michael, Your Grace." I have a feeling this is Bastille. Even if she isn't, Your Grace seems a polite way to greet this woman if I wanted to keep on her good side.

"Are you lost, Michael?"

"No. I was actually taken here as a prisoner by your le... subjects." I *was* going to say legions, but that's probably not the best thing to say to a Demon-Queen.

"I see." Then her disposition surprises me. "Zieetaaas-ah!"

I hear fumbling footsteps, as Zietas crashes into the wall of the tunnel. He straightens himself, and clears his throat. "You summoned me into your presence, Great One?" He bows, keeping his eyes averted from her.

"Yes, what can you tell me about this young man?"

Zietas snarls silently at me. "Probably just some tyke who got lost and tumbled into this cavern, Great One. I'll take him off your hands?"

"That's not what he told me. This young man told me he was taken here as a captive? Do you know anything?"

"I know, yesterday some of my men were enthralled, they snatched a bloke mucking around your Division Fire yesterday. One of them must have brought him here."

Bastille turns to me, asking how I could see the Shadow Flames.

"I can see the fire because," I pause for just a second then plunge into the truth, "Uli's blood runs through my veins!" I realize what I said, and cuss like a sailor. Bastille puts a hand on my shoulder, and turns back to Zietas.

"You know how I feel about lying Zietas. Now tell me, is this the boy you told me you slew by the Koolivoo Waterhole?"

"It is, my Queen."

"I see, so that means you did not slay his sister either, correct?" Zietas affirms her. "Tell me Zietas, why didn't you slay them, when I gave you an order to do so?"

"Desoto, my Queen. He wanted to see the girl, I reckon her name was Amber, face another thylacine in exchange to let them go free."

"And you agreed to this?" Bastille asks. Zietas nods reluctantly. "I don't care if Desoto requested the girl to face a Megalania, you went against an order Zietas, and you know I don't take kindly to those who do not follow my orders. So, because you lied to me, what should be your punishment?" She places one of her hands in the folds of her robe, and it emerges as a thin, multi-jointed leg with a talon on the end.

"Do what you see fit, my Queen," a slight tone of nervousness peeks through his voice. Zietas closes his eyes.

"Very well, but I want your eyes open so you can see your torture." She turns to me. "You may choose to watch or not."

Deciding to witness Bastille make an example of Zietas is something I wish I *had* turned my back upon. In one movement, she jabs his eye with the leg and plucks it out, but Zietas only grunts softly. If she did that to me, I'd scream in agony for a solid two minutes. I begin to wonder if this bloke feels any pain, but Bastille doesn't stop there. She pulls the eye from the leg and hands it to him, commanding him to eat it. Zietas complies, and I turn my face, suppressing the urge to chunder.

Then, it's over.

Bastille shoves Zietas to the ground and tramples him as she walks down the tunnel. Halfway she stops. "You are to seek out Michael's sister and bring her to me. I want her body moribund, so she can be broken easier."

Then the witch disappears around a corner and the sound of her walking fades to silence. Zietas shrouds his eye with his hood. He turns his face to me, blood creeping down his right cheek. He swipes at it and blood smears his cheek as he stands.

"Your sister will pay for this, mate!"

CHAPTER 2 A Jonah Story of Simpsons Gap

AMBER

SUNLIGHT BATHES THE ROOM in a yellow glow as the sun rises bringing a new day. Though my vision is blurry, I can make out some objects.

Across the room is what I believe to be a wardrobe, and beside me is a night table. I blink, and my vision clears, so I try to step from the bed. Pain shoots through my chest, forcing me to lie back against the pillow. My confrontation with Zietas, if you could even call it that, replays in my head, and I mull over it.

I didn't even graze him! Well, no, there was that time I nicked his finger, but everything else I threw at him, he countered, and kept me to the ground. Surely though, a person cannot be that good in combat. Can they?

I brush my hair from my face. "How long was I out?"

"Three days." A voice says from the door. My eyes dart to the sound as an elderly, aborigine man stands in the doorway. "My apologies for startling you, Amber."

I give the man a fake grin. Tonelessly, I ask, "How do you know my name?"

"I know more than your name. I know that the reason you lost your battle with that man was because you were overconfident."

I stare at the ceiling, blowing at a stray strand of hair, and my clothing flops off my shoulder. That's when I realize, I'm not wearing my shirt, but a wet tank-tunic, and another piece of clothing that I find embarrassing.

"Let's clear up a few fog patches. The reason I lost against Zietas was because I hadn't eaten for sixteen hours. If I'd eaten more than just a granola bar, I would have been better nourished to take him. It had nothing to with overconfidence. Besides, my brother wounded him! That's gotta count for something, right?"

The man moves his hips from side to side probably pondering my response. After a few seconds, I regret saying it.

I try to sit up, but the pain returns to my chest. I remember Zietas slashing my side, but did he break a rib as well?

"I suggest you stay in that bed for another day whiles that wound of yours heals." Hold the phone, how did he know about... my jaw

146

drops in abhorrence. "Relax, child, my daughter bandaged you. Alira?"

Alira pokes her head in the door smiling at me. Golden hair, lowlighted with brown accentuates her cinnamon face and chestnut colored eyes. Her facial features are flat, and broad as aborgine's often are, but she was fair complexioned. Alira steps in the doorway. She's definitely fit, and about my age. The blokes at Indro would definitely give her a second gander.

"How ya goin'?" I ask, casting her a fake smile.

"I'm fine, and it is great to see you're finally awake, Amber."

My face flushes, as Alira giggles sitting on my bed. She puts a hand on the sheets. Her grin becomes a concerned expression. "Father came just in time. That follower of the demon was ready to take you away."

I wish Zietas had taken me, at least that way I would be with Michael.

If Talo did not come to you when he did, you would have seen your brother for two seconds, and then your cause would be lost, because Bastille would have either recruited you or taken your life.

On the flip side of that pessimistic statement, I'd be with Michael, however short that time may be.

I purse my lips, longing for this voice just to let me alone, but I reckon that isn't happening. Talo casts me a questioning scowl. Apparently, he believes I directed the sneer towards him.

"Sorry, my side just hurts." I lie. Sure, it's wrong, but it's better than admitting I hear a voice in my head isn't it? Talo and Alira have been so hospitable, why turn them off with such a peculiar statement?

Talo smiles and vacates the doorway, while his daughter acquaints herself with me. I really don't feel up to talking, but why be hostile to her, especially since she took the time to bandage my wounds.

"Alira? Come here, please?" Talo calls from down the hall somewhere.

Alira raises a finger and steps out to aid her father. I take the time to examine the bandaging. Alira wrapped my waist in bandages, and my eyes fall to the large, black stain on the bandages. Zietas ripped a descent wound in my side.

I lay back on the bed, sighing. Inactivity and I butt heads. Unless I'm sleeping, I don't like remaining idle. Still, seeing as I *am* idle, I take in the room a little more, and reckon it is Alira's. On her dresser, a handmade sock doll hugs a bean-stuffed dog. The scene cracks a smile. I remember those days.

My hosts knock on the door, and my gaze turns to it, the smile still on my face. Talo and Alira enter. Alira holds a pot of tea, I reckon. Talo whisks a bowl of caperbush in a broth. (Mum makes this on occasion when she doesn't feel like cooking).

"Eat, you need the strength." Talo says.

I take the spoon and dig into the tangy fruit pulp lined with black seeds. A lot of tourists call it passion fruit, but according to Michael, passion fruit is sweeter in taste. Alira pours me a cup of tea. I thank her then my hosts leave me to eat.

My mind wanders to Michael. I pray Bastille doesn't do away with him before I get to him. Then again, where am I, and how far is he from wherever Talo and Alira live? I call for Talo. He comes to door, concern on his face.

"Do you not like the food?" He asks.

"Oh no, the food's ace," I wince at my habit of using Strine. Talo waits for my requests. "I just wanted to know where I am."

"My house, just outside of Simpson's Gap. If you look out your window you can see it in the distance."

Of course. That's where that voice told me to head. Suddenly, I feel like that Jonah bloke from the Bible.

See, Jonah, was told by God to preach in some city. (Nineveh was it?) Anyway, he decided to take a boat in another direction. A storm blew in. He said God sent the storm because he disobeyed him. Then Jonah told the sailors that if they threw him overboard, the seas would calm. Don't ask me why he knew this would happen, but it did. The sailors went along with it after lightening their cargo holds, and the storm still did not cease. You probably know the rest, a fish swallows him and, he lives inside it for three days repenting to God. The fish spits him out a few days' walk from the city, and Jonah finishes the task God called him to do originally.

The light bulb glares. My *storm* was Zietas, because I sought the source of the Shadow Flames instead of going to Simpsons Gap. My *fish*, lying unconscious for three days, and my city to preach at was essentially Simpson's Gap. Although, my missionary work is to learn whatever The Voice instructed me to learn here, so that I may be equipped to take on Bastille.

I'll admit, the whole idea of solely facing a power-mongering demon alone sounds, well, difficult.

I glance out the window. The sun makes the two rounded peaks of the pass blaze like red-hot coals in the distance. I turn back to my food and nibble away at it. The food is filling, and I realize how hungry I am. Three days in a coma does that to a person I guess. My fork stabs what looks to be chicken. I bring it to my mouth, and tear off a piece. Galah cooked over a fire. The flavour's amazing, so I wolf down the poultry and want more, but refrain from asking. I do not want to appear ungrateful.

Alira enters the room and sits on the bed. She has this questioning look on her face.

"What's up?" I ask, covering my mouthful of food.

"How did you do it?"

"Do what?"

"Escape the shadows. Father says he saw you stumble from the shadows, while he was out bagging that Galah. How did you do it?"

"I'm not quite sure what you mean by that, Ali."

"You came out of the fire. Were you placed in there to stop it, or did you make a mistake and go in?"

I try to explain how I wound up in the Shadow Flames as best I can. As she listens to my story her eyes widen, and I reckon she could burst into tears at any given moment. When I finish, she is speechless.

"You are brave," she finally says.

"Michael sacrificed himself for me." I swallowed hard. "I only did what needed to be done, but I wasn't quick enough. He got sucked into the flames. However, I won't lose hope, for as long as I have hope, I can save him and stop Bastille."

Alira stares at me; she puts a hand to her forehead stands and paces the room. "Yakgarra!" I hear her breathe.

Yakgarra indeed. It means wow in Wagiman, and my peers have caught me saying it a few times. I know Wagiman words because I want to have a full conversation with my grandmother one day. We call her Juju, short for Abuju.

"You have lots of devotion. I don't know if I would be able to do what you did."

"He is my twin. I have to rescue him. I shared a womb with him, grew up by his side for fifteen years. You could say we're inseparable."

It was this loyalty that drove me to bandage his wounds. This loyalty is why he sacrificed himself for me. Alira would never understand the bond Michael and I share.

I watch her leave, and lay back against the pillow. My wound burns, but sleep overtakes me. I know I should get up and move around a little, but I'm still recovering.

One more day. I'll wait one more day. After all, I'm not going anywhere. That Voice has brought me here, and it is here I will stay until it tells me I am ready to confront Bastille.

CHAPTER 3 The Adder's Venom

AMBER

"RISE AND SHINE AMBER," says Talo, as he raps on my door.

I peek out from the sheets, gazing out the window; the moon hangs on the horizon. Why is he waking me this early? I'm never up this early... ever! Sure, I can get up in the morning, but before the first rays of the sun? That's pushing it, even for me. However, Talo does not tell me. Instead, he tosses me my gauntlets and I understand. Today, I start training to face Bastille. Whining, I roll over, draw up the sheet, and face the wall. Silence. Melodious, silence. I lull myself back to sleep. One more hour. One more hour, then I'll start my training.

A thylacine yips dangerously close. I'm instantly bolt-upright in bed; I whip on my gauntlets, and scan the room. Another scream crumbles into a giggling fit. Alira stands in the doorway. She's holding some clothing, unable to contain herself.

"You're a riot, Ali." I say.

"Sorry, Father said it would wake you up."

155

Well, he was right. I'm awake. Awake and dreading the idea of rising before the sun. Do these two live on a farm? The only person I know who gets up this early is my mother, even then, I reckon she rises at five, not two hours after midnight.

"Today you meet your mentor." Alira says excitedly.

"My mentor?"

"Yes, he came to our door last night wondering how you were. We told him you were asleep and that he should come back tomorrow morning. He'll probably be here soon. His name was Desoto or something like that?"

I purse my lips struggling to keep the lid on my pot of boiling water. I must still be half-asleep, because there's no way Desoto is my mentor! How can that doubting coward be my mentor? Besides the bloke follows Bastille. I fall back against the pillow, staring at the ceiling. Alira steps into the room. Half following her with my eyes, she places my clothing on the bed, smiles, and closes the door behind her as she walks out.

I want to continue sleeping, but Alira may just scream next time, so I throw back the covers, and step from the bed stretching. My feet touch the floor, and they tingle from the cold. I switch on the lamp and examine the clothing: Tree Leaper attire. This has to be a cruel joke. Probably a present from Zietas, reminding me he still has my brother. I throw on my Capris instead. You couldn't pay me a hundred dollars to wear that clothing. I tug a brush through my lengths then get it out of my face with a head band.

Handmade living room furniture and a dining room suite greet me when I step out of the room. Over the mantel is a picture of Talo pecking with a Caucasian woman, while she wraps her arms around a beaming, younger Alira. I smile at the photograph. Then, I flop to the couch gazing at the plaster ceiling.

"You don't like the clothing?" Alira asks.

I tilt my head to look her in the eye. Feeling awkward, I roll over, resting my arms on the back of the couch, "I'm not wearing it because it reminds me of my battle with Zietas."

"Oh," her face droops only for a second the a smile brightens her face. "Want some breakfast?"

"Yes, please."

Alira beckons me into the kitchen and slides a plate of eggs and two Cheesymite Scrolls to me. Alira stands by seeking feedback on how she did. I cannot say I don't want the scrolls because I might offend her, but... it's Vegemite. Still, I bite into the scroll to show her I'm grateful for the meal. The Vegemite hits my tongue and I press my fingers against my lips. I manage to swallow the wad of food. Alira's hand reaches in and grabs the plate.

"I'm not a fan of the paste, either. I only thought that because you were from the big city that you missed Vegemite. Would you care for toast with marmalade instead?"

"If it's not too much trouble."

A few minutes later Alira sets two pieces of toast and marmalade in front of me. She joins me just as Talo walks in through the door, wiping his hands on a rag.

We greet each other good morning, and he asks me how my side is fairing today. Honestly, I haven't looked at it since I woke, so I tell him it's healing. Talo smiles and takes a scroll from the bench. Leaning against the bench, he savours the scroll as best he can, before reaching for the other one. I turn my focus on my toast.

A heavy, rather demanding knock startles me out of my seat.

"He's early." Talo says, wiping his hands on his shirt. He heads for the door. I hear it squeak open then Talo says in a growling sort of tone, "You're not Desoto, so what are you doing here?"

I tune into the conversation. "Don't compare me to that traitor! Where's the girl?"

I freeze, and break into a cold sweat. Alira glances at me. She doesn't need an explanation. My horrified expression tells her everything, and she points to the back door of the kitchen. As quietly as I can, I slide under the table and crawl across the floor to my escape. My ears are still tuned to the conversation.

"I'm sorry, but it is only my daughter and me who live here."

"You take me for a fool, mate? I know she's here, because I remember you."

"I'm sorry, but I do not know who you are talking about, perhaps a description?"

"Perhaps this will help." Metal shrieks as Zietas removes his sword. I reckon he is probably holding it against Talo's throat.

I take a gander at Alira. Her eyes are wide with fear, and she has every right. Her father is at knifepoint. I reckon he's all she has left because I never heard her mother come in last night or leave this morning.

My hand grasps the door and I turn the knob. The door creaks loudly. I push it open and close it. I suddenly realize, as my feet hit a puddle, that my knapsack is still inside. Forget my knapsack. I need to get away from here.

Then I realize my gauntlets are still inside, and to confront Bastille without those, well... I shudder at that thought. Besides, I cannot just run off and let Zietas slay my hosts. That would be cowardly. So, I sneak around the house and ready myself on the balls of my feet. I perform a basic jump kick breaking the glass of the window to Alira's room. Zietas bursts through the door, but he doesn't leap for me. Instead, face boiling in rage, he storms down the hall poising his scimitar.

"You liar!" He bellows.

Part of me wants to run, but as I said I can't let these two die, so with that mindset I grab my blades and walk down the hall.

Alira's horrified, mournful scream splits the air. I rush down the hall. A struggle rages within the kitchen. Talo throws dishes and shields himself with a chair, and though Zietas overpowers him, Talo is certainly fending Zietas off better than I could. Somehow, he finds time to tell Alira and me to run. I hold my ground and fire at Zietas, but Talo continues to order us to the door.

"Father I..."

"Alira, I order you to go with Amber! You will be safer with her than if you were to stay here. Now go!"

I hold out my hand to Alira. She doesn't take it, but watches Talo pin Zietas with a chair for a second.

In that split moment, Talo pushes his daughter at me, "Get out of my sight! That's an order, Alira." Ordering her to get out of his sight. Talk about harsh hooroos.

Alira's eyes well with tears as she buries her face in her hands. I'm not having that. Run and

137

cry another day. I drag at her hand then she tears out into the breezy, dark morning with me following close behind. The sounds of the fight fade on a whispering breeze.

We head north into Simpson's Gap, and there we breathe. I hold the side Zietas slashed, and lift the tunic to check the bandages. Alira drops to the ground, sobbing. My gaze turns back through the pass. The horizon dwarf's Talo's house, and from it, clouds of thick smoke billow into the heavens. My blood boils, and my breath slows. Zietas, you are a miserable man!

Then, I realize Alira is crying softly. She sat on her knees, eyes welling with tears. I squat and console her. She looks at me as if asking for my permission to cry, but then she bawls into my shoulder anyway. I wrap my arms around her. Only Zietas would involve the innocent in *our* conflict. Are there any depths he will not sink in order to turn me over to Bastille?

A sigh reaches my ears. "The pit of evil runs eternally deep for those who submit their lives to the Centipede. There is no depth to which they can sink, because they've already sold their soul."

I fire a blade toward the voice. A hooded man deflects the blade with two swords. A Tree Leaper. I rush him, and he reveals his identity. Desoto. I stop dead and glare at him. Alira stands at my side. Yet there's something different about him. The once fearful eyes now radiate with a deep sense of peace. Desoto beckons us to follow him.

"You expect me to just follow you, when I know you were once a follower of Bastille?"

"I cannot tell you to do anything, Amber. The choice must be yours as it was mine. By now, you realize this task is impossible for you to complete in your own strength."

What does he mean by the choice must be mine? What choice? The choice to follow him into a potential ambush? Then I lose this war before I even begin it. Zietas may advertise his intentions on a billboard, but I'm certain that is not the way of every Tree Leaper. For all I know, Desoto could be the greatest con artist in Bastille's ranks. I pick up the blade he countered, and take a seat on a rock defiantly, setting my bag down.

"You say you've made a choice? What choice?"

"I made a choice to follow the truth and turn from the lie. Truth you must also find if you hope to have any chance of rescuing your brother."

"I thought this was training to spar with Bassie and Zietas."

"That *is* part of it, but the Centipede uses suggestion to attack."

I want to question what that means. Before I can ask, Desoto reads the puzzlement in my expression.

"Allow me to explain. Everyone has fears, shortcomings, and selfish whims. The Centipede taps into these, subduing and seducing you with them. For me it was my cowardly nature. She promised me courage, and the ability to overtake all who stood in my way. The truth of the matter was that she never healed the fault. In the end, I was still a coward. It was this realization that woke me up from the indoctrination, and I saw her for who she really was: a fraud.

"I sought other means to free myself from my shortcomings. Then, I heard a voice. It encouraged me, gave me a peace I'd never felt before. *Come to me... you who are weary and burdened, and I will give you rest*, it said.

"So, I sought after this hope, while playing the mindless drone for as long as I could until the day when the voice told me to leave. I slipped out one night, and was given the task to train you. So now you know my story, and what the Centipede is capable of, do you really wish to take her on alone?"

I still don't know who this Centipede is, but somehow I know there is truth to what Desoto says. "All right, you got a deal, Des," I say standing, "but one slip up or one hint that I reckon you're plotting with other Tree Leapers, and I leave!"

Alira stands too, but she seems to have been waiting for me, almost as if she hungered for these tactics so she could solely defeat Zietas. Maybe, thereby avenging her father, but if she wants Zietas, I'm okay with that. So long as I get Michael back, and *we* slay Bastille (and this Centipede) together, I'm good with that.

Desoto nods and beckons us to follow him. I shoulder my knapsack too quickly, and a sharp pain surges through my side. Right, I'm still healing. I'll have to start light. That way, I can heal properly and still train. Sure, it may take a little longer, but I don't want to be clutching my side when comes the fight.

Michael comes to my mind. Be safe mate, I want to tell him. Try not to be impetuous and do something you'll regret, he seems to be telling me.

We hike a narrow pathway ascending the east wall of the gorge. A couple of times Alira needs to steady my balance. All the while, Desoto trudges on in front of us. Half way up he tosses each of us a pair of gloves, which he calls Gecko Hands. I feel the fingers, and wonder if Desoto simply stretched the skin of a gecko over them. I assume the material is synthetic, because the other way is too cruel. Nonetheless, synthetic or not, Desoto wants me to wear them, so I might as well. I test them on the rock, they stick and don't let go. I tug. Still nothing.

"Roll your fingers." Desoto instructs.

I do and they come off easily. Intrigued, I try the sensation again. They are useful now. But what about in Bastille's domain when I'm clobbering her? Swapping out my only weapon for a pair of these leaves me open and therefore absurd. I hold up a gauntlet, and Desoto understands. Good, I can conserve my breath. He motions for the gauntlets, and I hand them to him.

Desoto studies the weapon, while I tap my foot and hum a ditty. He purses his lips. As if weighing them, he hefts the gloves and then scans between them and the gecko pair. I can almost see his brain wheels chugging and the steam billowing from his ears in thick clouds.

"Come on will ya! By the time you're done, Zietas will be dragging me back to Bastille."

Desoto looks up. "You're right, he will. Consider this part of your training." He tosses me everything, and I stumble backwards.

Alira reaches for my arm to hold me steady. She smiles, while I just glare at Desoto.

"Well, put 'em on and get climbing already."

I shove the gauntlets into my pack and yank on the Gecko Hands. Then I start my climb, while the lazy Desoto takes a path up to the top. He offers Alira to join him, but she prefers to climb with me. I feel like the hero, excuse me, the *heroine*, on some mystical quest, training from the elderly guru who sits in the shade sipping tea.

When we finally make it to the top Desoto presses on. After that climb with the injuries I had gloriously incurred, I reckon I deserve a break, don't you? Desoto turns to us and rushes me drawing his sword, forcing me almost over the cliff. My bag puts me off kilter, and my arms flail to keep my balance. Desoto grasps my arm and pulls me forward. I wrench free, and brush a lock of hair out of my face.

"What the heck was that for? I thought you were training me not trying to kill me!"

"I did. That was a test on how well you guarded yourself. You failed it." He says flatly.

I stare at him, a black look etched on my face.

"Squizz at me like that all you like Amber, my purpose is to train you not to babysit you. You are welcome to rest if you are tired, but guard yourself while doing so. The worst mistake you can make in battle is let your guard down as you just did."

"Whatever."

"Very well, when your attitude changes, then I'll train you. Drop your bag."

"Why?"

"Okay, don't drop it." Desoto rushes me and paralyzes me before I realize I'm on the ground. I slump to my knees and flop like a rag doll to the ground. Then he turns to Alira. "It's Ali right?"

"Alira, but Ali is fine."

"Ali, would you carry Amber's bag for her, please?"

"Cannot she carry it?"

"No, I have paralyzed her with a technique called the Adder's Venom. I learned it when I was young. She will not be moving until she is ready to train."

Grouse now and I'll never reach Michael!

I try to push myself to my feet, but my body gives out, and I collapse to the ground again. Alira removes my bag and Desoto throws my limp body over his shoulder.

Every second I'm with this bloke, I remember why I despised him and Zietas. Both of them use tactics to drop me to my knees, and if Desoto is supposed to be training me, why is he paralyzing me? My head hurts from trying to connect the dots, so I drop it and blow at my bangs. Desoto isn't training me, he's pointing out my flaws, and he is wasting his breath, because I already know my shortcomings. He believes they have to do with combat skills, but they don't have anything to do with combat skills. I can take on Bastille. I just need earplugs.

Amber, why do you resist those I put in authority over you? You know why I have chosen Desoto to train you, he told you himself. He has lived in the darkness, so he knows its power. He is changed. He is a new creation in my name. If you cannot trust him, then trust me. Trust that I have placed him here for your benefit, so that you will not fall prey to the darkness.

There's that voice again, but for all I know it could be Bastille. Yet it hasn't steered me wrong so far, and it brought me here safely.

All right, I'll trust you to know what you're doing, whoever you are. You've taken me this far, so I guess I can trust you.

We arrive at Desoto's camp late in the afternoon. How he managed to carry me all this way is supernatural in itself, but he did, and here we are. He sets me down against a rock and pats my shoulder. Disdaining him, I gaze out across the gorge from the crevasse in the side of the wall. A grove of Eucalyptuses shrouds the entrance, and below is a small watering hole, which I reckon is salt water. He lights a fire while I strain to turn my neck away from it. The pain shoots through my body, so I just close my eyes and rest. I'll skip dinner tonight.

CHAPTER 4 Bastille's Enticing Juxtaposition

MICHAEL

AMBER HAUKSBY, MY SISTER, my fraternal half, and my closest friend. For fifteen years we grew up by each other's side. We laughed together, and we sparred together. She was my first choice for soccer, and I was usually her second. Sometimes, though on opposing teams, we would help each other out regardless of our peers' disapproval.

Even now, on this quest, miles apart, I know she is searching for me, or acquiring the necessary skills to free me from Bastille's prison, the very thing I am unable to do. However, with my wounds still hindering me, it takes all my effort to even raise a leg to perform a basic sidekick. Though, I must keep trying. I owe her that much. She persevered to fight the thylacines, when I was down. She bandaged my wounds, keeping me alive; she wanted to take on Zietas, Desoto and Ira in her wounded state. Yes, not trying would disgrace her.

I stand in the ready position, trying thrice over to make a single, decent kick. Running and leaping into the air also borders on difficult. So,

I decide the best course of action is to wait for the furrows to heal. This way, I increase my chances of performing better, and reduce risking further injury.

Footsteps echo through the tunnel. I take the defensive stance. The orange glow of a torch flicks on the wall, and I brace to kick. A Tree Leaper comes into view. In the glow of the torch, I gaze upon the stark, blank expression of the woman. Instinctively, I realize that somewhere in that face, my potential future haunts me.

I recognize the woman. She wanted to slay Amber and me in the clearing, but Zietas silenced her. What was her name? Harmy? No. Sally? No, it definitely starts with an 'H'. Hol? Yes, that is her name. Hol, which is probably short for Holly.

Hol pauses in front of me. The torch light reflects off the rocky walls and flickers over her face. She says, blandly, "Her Greatness requires an audience with ya. I've been instructed to bring ya by any means necessary, so either you can walk beside me or I'll club ya one, and carry ya. Your choice."

I do not enjoy the idea of having this woman club me over the head with a blunt object particularly, so I walk beside her. That decision brings my sister to mind. She would stand up to Hol, and probably wind up unconscious because she would not comply with the request. I may be headstrong, but I know when I'm powerless. Sure, I could pick up a rock and heave it at Hol's head, but it hurts to stand, let alone walk. No harm in seeing what goes.

Hol guides me through the winding network of tunnels, and I lose sight of her on several occasions. I don't dare ask her to slow her pace because I'm afraid she will just club me over the head and carry me. Everything about her intimidates me, from her stocky build to her gruff voice and blank expression, but especially the two daggers jingling on her belt. Unarmed, I decide making her cranky may not be the wisest choice.

We enter a large antechamber, but it's not Bastille's quarters. A perpetual haze rests in the air, as a dozen or so torches illuminate the room. Hol welcomes me to the main room of the Nest. I reckon that's what *her greatness'* domain is called. The smoke fills my lungs and I cough. Perhaps this is why the man Amber found had a grey face. He breathed this every day. Hol snaps her fingers in my face then tosses me a pair of climbing claws. She points to a shaft above me.

"Bastille's up there waiting for ya. Get going, I have things to do."

"Wouldn't it be easier if you gave me a personal escort?" I stall.

"I can heave this at ya, if you'd like?" She picks a rock off the ground and tosses it.

I decide to drop the subject. Climbing to the shaft is the easy part. What I dread, is hauling myself into the hole because I'm claustrophobic. I look down. That's a mistake.

Normally, I revel in the thrill of hanging from the ceiling of rock faces, but only when secured in belaying equipment. This, on the other hand is terrifying. Firstly, I am in a cave, and secondly, to crawl into the hole will force me to clamber across the ceiling of this cave like a bat.

I take a deep breath as a drop of sweat plummets to the floor below. I can almost see it splash, break apart roll into the nooks of the floor. One wrong move and that sweat drop will be me. Hol bailed too, so I cannot ask her for assistance. Another deep breath, and I scramble into the hole.

137

The passage narrows, and the fear of getting stuck overwhelms me. I stop. Then a hand reaches down to pull me from the shaft. I reach for it, and realize I grabbed the hand of Bastille. She smiles at me and beckons me to sit with her on her throne. I glance around. Veins of opal streak the walls and ceiling. Torches cast bright red halos about the sandstone, but the centerpiece of the room is Bastille's throne carved from a single opal. I stare awestruck. It is at least one-hundred times bigger than the largest opal excavated, which was one-thousand carats!

"Beautiful, isn't it?" Bastille asks caressing the stone.

I keep my response to myself. But I know she sees the awe in my gaze.

Bastille ushers me to the throne, and I willingly go, afraid she'll remove my eye as well if I don't comply. Yet, everything she does composes a symphony of serenity. "There's no need to be shy with me Michael, I mean only to talk."

She takes a seat on the throne and pats it. I glance around to see if Amber may burst from the shaft; disappointed by her absence, I take a seat. Bastille smiles.

"You miss your sister," she says. "I can tell. The two of you must have been very close."

"You have no idea."

"Do not fret over her void, soon you will be reunited with her, but for the interim, why don't you hone your combat skills here with me, and when the two of you meet again, you can show her how you've grown. After all, we wouldn't want another humiliation like that thylacine incident would we?"

My gaze shifts to her smiling face. How does she know about that?

"Yes, Michael, I know all about your encounter, and how your sister slew three of the four beasts. I know also that while you admire her abilities you also envy them, and rightfully so. You are a young man, and it is in your nature to seek gratification in conquest. Alas, your sister has always surpassed your combative skills hasn't she?"

I nod. Amber always managed to master the techniques of Taekwondo quicker than me.

"You already know you are smarter than she is, and she knows it too, but she will never openly admit this to you. She has too much pride. I can teach you to become a better warrior, and even outrival her."

Outrival Amber? That would be a feat, but could Bastille really do it? For once, Amber would be the one pinned, and I would land all the kicks and jabs.

The proposal gets me thinking. Maybe Bastille isn't as bad as Maliu made her out to be. Perhaps she is not a demon at all, and Maliu is. After all, he sent us out into the Never Never to take on a demon and destroy the Shadow Flames. His devious plan fooled Amber and me. What better way to conceal your intentions than for people to believe you are the hero?

Bastille is offering to train me, enhance my skills. Maliu just sent us out with no preparations to die. Surely, if Uli sent him as a messenger, he should train us first, shouldn't he?

"I'll take up your offer, but I have one request."

"Anything you like."

"You keep my sister alive when she is brought here."

"That can be met."

I nod, and step to the floor. I'm eager to start my training. Bastille approves of my enthusiasm and sends for someone she calls Ira. I smile at her, but she nods with her expression shuttered.

"Ira is one of my greatest warriors. She will teach you all you need to know."

Ira nods and beckons for me to follow her. She leads me through another narrow tunnel to a room with a spring. A pale light glimmers off the pool's surface. Opal creeps across the walls like tree roots reaching for water.

My eyes return to the pool, and lying on the bottom is a halved, refined opal, twice the size of Bastille's throne. I wonder how gems this large have not been discovered. Then I see a skeletal hand under one of the halves and a pickaxe resting beside it. Someone did discover the stone and attempted to mine it. For a moment, I mourn for the poor soul.

In one corner of the room towers a shimmering crystalline wall. My reflection stares back at me, and suddenly I feel touchy about my appearance. I look too scrawny, so I try imagining myself with a toned body, not too much, but just enough that I would be stronger than Amber. Hopefully, Bastille's training will give me these results.

Ira clears her throat, and turns to walk out telling me to cleanse myself in the spring. I hesitate. Bastille didn't say anything about cleansing myself. Ira re-enters the room.

"It's just a bath, nothing too obscene, but you must cleanse yourself if you wish to join the ranks."

I did not want to join the ranks. I wanted to train, and just to *seem like* I joined the ranks. But then I also did not want to disappoint Bastille. She was so kind to me when I met with her in her throne room, and it seemed right to give her something back, so I acknowledge Ira with a nod.

"I'll be back with your clothing." She leaves.

An evil presence crushes the air around me. The air in the chamber instantly feels heavy, but I feel light headed. The ardour of serenity that had enveloped me since Bastille had grasped my hand and hauled me into her chamber evaporates. Dropping to my knees, I hold my head struggling to quell the throbbing in my head. My legs quiver then my head feels like lead. I shuffle back from the edge for fear of falling in. That's another thing. Fear consumes me. When I was with Bastille I felt safe, but here everything appears to be reaching for me.

The veins of opal swirl into mockeries of living animals: a dingo, a death adder, a frilled lizard. They all leer at me, eyes shining with anticipation and villainy. I shut my eyes and rock on my heels hoping they will be gone when I open them again.

I allow my eyes to ease open, the water shimmers before me. Then Amber pops up from the water. Her sudden appearance sends me reeling backwards towards the crystalline wall. She wears a flowing, white gown.

Amber looks at me quizzically. "Come on, Michael, join me." She back strokes around the pool, further encouraging me to join her.

I shake my head.

She stops and tilts her head, "Why? What's holding you back?"

My mind races, thoughts swirling. Did Bastille capture her as well? That doesn't make sense. The last place I saw my sister was at the Shadow Flames right before the kamodo snagged my foot, and even if she had been taken prisoner, I would have seen her in the tunnel, right?

Perhaps she was captured and already bathed. What am I saying? Amber would rather die than agree to follow Bastille! Maybe she has died, and I'm seeing her ghost. Then again, her ghost would probably be at my side warning me not to go into the pool. I conclude this cannot be Amber.

I turn my back to the pool and see a faint silhouette stretched across the crystal rock. Call me crazy, but the silhouette looks like Amber only this one appears to be warning me not to get in the pool. The very thing I thought the Amber in the pool should be doing. The silhouette flails its arms around and seems to push against the wall.

"What are you looking at Mike?" Amber says from behind me. "There is no one there."

I blink and rub my eyes, but the silhouette remains.

It pounds on the rock, and a chilling realization arcs across my brain. What if it's not Amber? What if it's some creature trying to break free? Suddenly a little red patch of blood appears on the wall slowly dripping down it.

In a panic, I jump into the pool. Suddenly the waterborne-Amber's face turns grey. Her eyes blacken and her hair thins. The demon lunges at me trying to hold me under. When I surface I scream for help, and I scream my sister's name a few times. All the while, the silhouette continues to beat on the wall, probably trying to come to my aid.

Doubt evaporates, and I despise myself for mistaking a demon for my sister. My efforts to shake her wane, as Evil-Amber holds her grip. With the sixth dunk, my world goes dark.

CHAPTER 5 The Nine Traits of Light

AMBER

DESOTO JOSTLES ME AWAKE as the first rays of morning peek into the cave. Forgetting about my paralysis, my brain tells my body to sit bolt upright, but the muscles just tense and blood shoots to my head causing circular rainbows to dapple before my eyes. Tears flood my face, and I let Desoto console my anguish. Unable to move, I let him pat my back. Then another pain comes to my attention.

My knuckles. Blood drips from ruptured skin. Desoto bandages the wounds, as another hand squeezes my shoulder. Softly, over my lamentations, Alira sings a lullaby. The song (though in her native tongue) soothes my sorrow.

Tears subsiding, I sit there against the rock. A nightmare replays in my head. Michael, my analytical brother, is looking at me then turns mistaking a doppelganger for me. He sees me bang on the wall over and over and over I'm pounding on that wall. But in fear, he leaps into a black pool. He screams for me to rescue him from his mistake as Evil-me holds him under the water. Meanwhile, I pound on a crystalline barrier separating us in a futile attempt to reach him. Tears pool in my eyes. Then he vanishes from my view as I drag my fists down that impervious wall. I finally sink in defeat.

Desoto's eyes widen when I tell him my nightmare. "I know that pool. Bastille calls it the Spring of Rebirth, but it's really a watery pit of death. I think your nightmare was a vision. A horrific one at that, but still a vision, and I fear it's one of past events."

I lower my head as best I can, my eyes welling again. If Michael's already been in that pool, I don't want to think about the horror he's going through. Desoto must have seen my heartache, because he told me there is a hope. I look up, a longing in my eyes.

"Yesh is the way Amber. He has helped you this far, even if you don't realize it. He delivered you from the thylacines, and spared you when you confronted Zietas. He brought you here when Zietas burnt down Alira's home.

"Darkness looms on Australia's horizon, Amber, what is your choice?"

"Well, I could say to heck with you, but then Michael would still be in bondage, and Bastille will use the Shadow Flames in a twisted plot and, " I remember to breathe."What do I have to do?"

Desoto smiles, releasing me from the Adder's Venom.

My training starts with understanding Yesh, and what he wants for me. Desoto suspects he communicated with me because Uli may have known him. The story begins to intrigue me, and for the first time, I actually listen to the bloke. Desoto wields his words like a potter moulds clay. They roll off his tongue like a babbling stream, carefully planned, easily followed, and refreshingly true.

I take a quick gander at Alira. She, too, is entranced by Desoto's way of speaking. I can almost hear Yesh speaking in his head as he does mine. His lips simply reiterate the message, not tripping up his tongue.

Suddenly, Desoto stands and throws my gauntlets to me. The blades adhere to one another, but they look like my gauntlets. A smile eases across my lips. He took my gauntlets and somehow grafted them to the Gecko Hands, so I decide to call them Gecko Blades.

(Or rather Geckos because I'm lazy.) He must have done it while I was sleeping, and he beckons me to try them out. I hesitate, as I'm still recovering from my confrontation with Zietas.

"Can we start with something a little easier? Zietas really did a number on me." I show him the bandaged gash. "You know target practice, and what not."

"That's definitely Zietas' work, so I suppose we could start with the Nine Traits of Light."

Given everything that has happened, I reckon I know what these Nine Traits of Light could be, but I let Desoto explain them just to be sure.

They turned out to be what I thought: love, joy, peace, forbearance, compassion, benevolence, loyalty, clemency, and self-restraint. I'm not sure how these will help me checkmate Bastille and free my brother from bondage to her. I ask, but this time carefully choosing my words. Even then, my words have an edge to them. I cringe at them, but Desoto smiles forgivingly.

"I'll let you and Yesh work that one out. Shall we continue with your suggestion of accuracy?"

I nod, for it beats scrambling across the low ceiling of the cave.

"May I practice as well?" You know that anticipating look a child gives you when they want you to say yes? Well, Alira's face lights up the crevasse with that expression.

Desoto stalls. His dilemma is the centerpiece of an exhibit. Alira has no weapon. Desoto looks around. Then he vacates the premises promising he will return.

Alira follows him out and stands at the mouth. Her hand reaches for her face and sweeps. She's crying, and I know why.

How would you feel in this situation? Your father, struggling for his life against some psychopath, orders you to flee with a stranger into the Outback. He tells you he'll be fine, yet you have this gnawing notion in your noggin that he's only trying to console you. Still, you can hope, right? Then even that flame flickers out, because you see your house burning to the ground on the horizon.

I don't know about you, but I would certainly be crying now, knowing I'm orphaned at fifteen. Feeling sympathetic for her, I walk over and put my arm around her. Alira rests her head on my shoulder, wiping her eyes. I want to tell her everything will be all right. The words won't bring her father back, though

"You wanna try these?" I ask removing my blades and changing the subject. "They may take your mind off Zietas for a while."

"No thanks. It's okay."

"If you don't mind me asking what happened to your mother."

"Mother was a nature researcher, she studied endangered species. She had an interest in Lake Eyre, and she spent most of her time there, sometimes as long as three days. When she stayed away four days one time, we thought she returned to Adelaide with the findings. Then a week passed, and we hadn't heard a word from her. Father started to worry, so he drove to Adelaide, but no one had seen her.

"On his drive back a troop of dogs ran in front of him. He said they had glowing green eyes and shadowy fur. Their mouths were...

bloody. He followed the trail and found a skeleton dressed in her clothing. That was two years ago."

I mourn with her, but her story contradicts Maliu's. Again, analyzing is Michael's bowl of rice, but Maliu hinted the Shadow Flames sprang up in Brisbane overnight. Yet Alira said her father saw them two years ago in the Lake Eyre Basin. Well, not exactly the flames but that description sounded suspiciously like thylacines to me. If Bastille wanted to wipe out civilization, why dip her flames into the most fragile ecosystem of Australia far away from where people are packed together in civilization?

Desoto returns in the late afternoon with two planks of wood. On them, he's carved the shape of a boomerang. Alira and I watch as he carves the indigenous weapon. He uses his dagger like a planer shaving and tapering the wood into a wing. I could see Michael crouching beside him studying Desoto's craftsmanship. The thought of which brings tears to my eyes, so I decide to practice on a Eucalyptus tree in the valley to keep from crying.

I try my luck at scaling the tree and firing at the ground. The hands grip, but my feet just slide on the bark. I remove my shoes and socks trying again, this time wrapping the narrow trunk with my feet, I climb into the branches rolling my fingers. A pair of these shoes would be handy too. Probably wouldn't hurt to ask either.

Squatting with one hand gripping the tree for balance, I point a gauntlet at the ground, and my hair falls in my face. I brush it behind an ear, and a spectacular scene draws my attention.

Below me, a stream trickles down the gully. The Outback's open plain peeks between the towering walls of red sandstone. In the distance, a smoke circle rises into the sky. Smoke signals? I scorn the thought. Back to reality, I tell myself.

I fire the blade like normal, and it sails into the dirt as Alira's boomerang hits the ground beside it. I jump from the tree. The clapping of hands reaches my ears, and I turn to face Desoto. The searing pain in my side makes me want to double over, but I stand trying to conceal it.

"An ace landing Amber, but you might wanna move out of the way, or come back up here!" Desoto hollers to me.

I give him a thumb up, and pick up my shoes and blade, which I place in the satchel. Assuming Alira wants her boomerang back, I grab that too. Then trudge the path to his little cave. Alira thanks me for retrieving her boomerang.

"No worries. But you know what people call a boomerang that doesn't come back?"

"A stick. I know, Father told me that once, or maybe it was Mother. It was one of them at least."

I chuckle, and having owned a boomerang as a tyke, I show her how to throw it. The boomerang returns halfway to me. "It's been a while."

Alira giggles.

"May I?" Desoto asks Alira for the other boomerang.

Alira gives it to him, and he pinches one end and throws it overhand against the wind flicking his wrist to release it. The boomerang sails in a perfect arc back to his hand.

"Now you try." He hands her the boomerang and guides her arm.

When it returns, her smiling face dims the sun. She throws it again. I let fly an unladylike laugh through my nose as a grin creases her face. I'm glad she is happy again, at least for now the pain from loss of her father is subdued, or so it seems.

I remember the Gecko feet. "Hey Des, how long do you reckon it'll take you to make me a pair of Gecko Shoes? You know these for my feet?"

"Not sure. Never made 'em before, because the hands were sufficient enough. But if you want a pair I could show you how to weave the material and you could make some yourself."

"How am I supposed to climb though? I tried on a tree in the valley and I just slid back down."

"But you climbed the tree didn't you?"

"Yeah, but I had to remove my socks to do it, and the climbing was slow. How do you climb into the trees like a monkey?"

"Speed takes practice, but remember how you climbed the rock wall?" I nod. "Well, a tree is no different. When your hands find the right place, your feet will follow. It takes practice, but that's what we're here to do isn't it? Try again."

I nod, returning to the valley. Michael. Remember Michael.

Don't just remember your brother, recite the Nine Traits as you climb. Recite them, and the inscription on your gauntlets.

At the base of the tree once more, I breathe. "One. Love." I leap at the tree." Two. Joy." I begin to climb. "Three. Peace. Four. Forbearance. Five. Compassion. Six. Benevolence. Seven," my hand grasps the nearest branch, "Loyalty. Eight. Clemency. Nine. Self-restraint." I haul myself into the branches and recite the inscription on my wrist guard.

It is not enough to simply know these and cast them out as trinkets of information. You must apply them to your life. Only then can you show your brother the change within yourself, and bring him back to you.

Hold the phone. Apply them to my life? I thought I was learning this to confront Bastille.

You faced Zietas without me, and he brought you to the brink of death. If he can do that, then how much more Bastille will do?

Yesh has a point. If he had not sent Talo for me, I'd be at the mercy of Bastille now.

"Heads up!" Desoto hollers from the cliff. I lean back and the boomerang whizzes in front of me. It clips a few leaves and circles to the ground behind the tree.

"Sorry!" I hear Alira call.

"No worries. I'll get it for you."

She thanks me, and I bring the boomerang back up to her. Perhaps she should try a different weapon. Something that can still be used as a projectile, but requires less skill. The words slip from my mouth and she takes the defense.

"You say I cannot use this?"

"No, that's not what I meant. It's just, a boomerang is *very* difficult to use. I mean, I took lessons, and I still have trouble throwing it." I try to remember gentleness and kindness as I talk to her, but the words, though true, nip at her self-esteem. Thank goodness, Desoto knew how to defuse the squabble.

"Amber speaks true words, Alira. You are quickly improving on your technique, but because time is against us, I must insist you try a different weapon. Keep the boomerangs as a souvenir."

I suggest a bow and arrow. They are portable (somewhat) and are the next best thing to a gun. They also take less time to load than *my* weapons. Alira asks if I have one.

"No, but I can make you one."

"Would you?"

I lay awake that night reciting the Nine Traits of Light to myself. Alira sleeps beside me, and I envy her a little. With no kangaroos to count jumping across the road, I decide to sneak out into the night. Perhaps a chat with Yesh will calm my restless mind. The idea of following him is foreign to me. I understand why I need to follow him, and why I need him. But for fifteen years, I have made it on my own. Well, I get council from my parents, but you know what I mean. I put on my gauntlets and exit the cave.

As I walk a little ways from the crevasse, someone mutters. Diving behind a bramble I breathe shallowly and listen. The words are difficult to make out. I glance around for anything I can hide behind. A small ledge spears the starry sky like an arrowhead. Perfect. I scale the cliff and breathe shallowly. Standing will give away my position, so I crawl on my stomach to the edge taking care to roll my fingers across the rock.

Eavesdropping is more difficult than I anticipate. Whomever I overheard talking has either moved on, or is looking for me. I swallow hard. I scoot back from the edge. Against the moon filled night sky, I'm a torch in a cave. Quickly, I clamber down into the shadows.

"Shouldn't you be sleeping?" asks a voice. I freeze. "Relax, Amber."

I turn swiftly, aiming with my gauntlets in opposing directions. Desoto steps from the shadows, his sword glinting. Probably reckons I'll shoot him, and if he kept silent, I would have. I lower my weapons.

"Can't sleep," I admit.

"Another nightmare?"

"Well, no. I have one thing on my mind, but it's keeping me awake. I just can't seem to follow this Light Spirit as you do. All my life

I've been independent, and now, it all seems so, so foreign to me.

"There are so many questions in my head too. Where do I start? How do I communicate with him properly? You know, questions."

Desoto clasps my shoulder. "You've already begun, and there is no special way to talk with him. Never think of it as slavery, but as servitude. My relationship with him is different from yours because my past is different.

"Remember, I served Bastille at one point and sought a way out, a way which he provided. I cannot say how he came to you, but you know, and he knows. That is what makes him so personable."

A smile creases my face. My anxiety lulls; my troubled spirit settles still as if in safe harbor. I may not have talked with Yesh directly, but I could hear his voice in the words Desoto spoke, and so I thank him.

Desoto ushers me back to the cave, and I allow him to wrap his arm around my shoulder as we walk back. I converse with Yesh following Desoto's advice. A sense of peace washes over me. Perhaps this is the peace of mind Desoto also feels.

CHAPTER 6 Coo–ee! Coo–aa!

MICHAEL

IRA SLIDES INTO MY QUARTERS, greeting me good morning. I stretch on the bed, returning the greeting. The bed is a simple pile of straw covered with silk. I know it doesn't sound like the most comfortable of places to lay your head, but I often sleep on the floor of my room in a pile of blankets, so to me it is.

Ira tosses me the fire-roasted flank of some animal, and my hands clasp the bone. I begin to gnaw at the browned flesh. It's gamey and gives my jaw a workout, but it is flavorful and nothing like I've ever tasted before.

"What is this? It's really good."

"Wallaby."

After a few more bites, I set the meat aside. I like a gnarly hunk of meat occasionally, but even this is a little much. Setting the bone down, I stand and wipe the grease and juice from my chin with the sleeve of my shirt. Then I rub my hands together.

"You may wanna finish that. Don't want guests in your quarters while you're taking a kip."

"Mice don't bother me."

"Not exactly what I meant, but it's your call mate. Oh, by the way, you're gonna want these." She reaches into her cloak and lobs my gauntlets to me polished like a mirror. My reflection looks back at me.

"You can gussy up later, today you start your journey to become a deadly solider for Her Majesty, Bastille."

"Great! When do I start?"

"Now." The tone in her voice instantly puts me on guard.

Ira leads me through the winding passages of the network. We pass several quarters, most of them vacant and mirror images of my quarters. Tunnels ascend, descend and fork. The map I picture is a huge tumbleweed. If this network of tunnels were stretched into a single line, I could probably outline Australia! The tunnel deaf ends at a cliff. My shocked exclamation echoes about the chamber as rocks clatter down a steep crag splashing into a pool.

"Coo-aa! Coo-ee!" Ira crows.

"Coo-ee! Coo-aa!" comes a reply.

Torches burst to life all around me, and what first appeared to be a barren chasm becomes a cavern lined with a high-ropes course speared by stalagmites. The ropes wrap columns and ascend to the ceiling where stalactites and curtains of rock would graze my head if I climbed that high.

Ira leaps from the ledge onto a sloping mesa before us and scrambles up it. She turns to face me, but I shake my head. Walking through the twisted passages of this hole is my limit. My fear of caverns creeps up my spine. I can barely suppress it. Cold perspiration dampens the back of my neck, face, and clothes.

Ira urges me, "Come on little bloke. There's just water below. You can't hurt yourself."

That much I know because I heard it, but the question remains: How far below, because I don't see it? I stand my ground. She cannot say, nor do anything that will make me jump this gap. Surely, we can start with something else like target practice for instance, accuracy, camouflage, anything but leaping over a pit to a sloping rock!

"Look, mate, you have two options. Jump or get knocked into the water by someone running around that bend. Just so you're aware, Bastille does not hold a ceremony for new recruits. Most of them don't even know you exist, and a good many of them are not forgiving. So what's it gonna be, mate? A brawl with some burly bloke, or a jump? I can stand here all day," she takes a seat on the slope, "you on the other hand may only have a few seconds to make up your mind."

"You have any belaying equipment?"

Ira scoffs. "You won't have any of that out in the field, so why use it here? Everything you see here you'll come across in the field in some form or another, with the exception of lighting, of course. You have your wind, your water, your burning forest. Everything."

I swallow and psyche myself up preparing to jump. A running start, that's what I need. There's no going back with one of those. It's either jump or fall because the momentum pitches me over the edge.

Footfalls echo through the tunnel, and I turn too late. A member of the Bastille's ranks collides with me, and we tumble into the pool. The plummet into the pool feels like minutes, though only a few seconds actually pass. My torso hits the water and ten thousand needles pierce my back at once. Resurfacing, while moaning from the pain, I see Ira covering her face with her hand. Then the person who knocked us into the water breaks the surface. Even in the dim light, I recognize him. The bloke Amber failed to interrogate by the lake.

Come to think about it, she's always had trouble with my gender. Rather pathetic, really. It will be a miracle if she ever decides to have a relationship. I chuckle.

"You think this is funny?" The man scowls. I didn't reckon his expression could get any more sour, but it does, as he points a finger. "You, you're that red-haired bloke I saw alongside that chick at Lake Koolivoo. Decided to infiltrate and conquer did ya? Well, your little excursion ends here!" He lunges for me, and I swim to the wall.

"Oy! Lepez!" Ira hollers from the cliff. Lepez scowls at her. "Leave him, he's bathed."

Lepez turns to me bowing as best he can in the water. "My apologies, mate, welcome to the ranks." He invites me to climb first so I do, and he follows.

On the ledge, he doesn't waste time with introductions, because we've already been acquainted, twice (though more formally the second time around). He offers his services and anything that will make me feel more at home. He extends a hand and I shake it. After that, he leaps across a mesh to another part of the course. I watch intrigued, until Ira taps me on the shoulder.

"Looks like you made a friend."

I smile at her.

Maliu is definitely wrong. These folks aren't out for blood, they're just good people following orders. Orders from a woman who just wants to cleanse the world of all the evil in it. I see nothing wrong with that. Sure innocents might be slain, too, but I'm sure Bastille will give them the option to live. She did with everyone in this cave. If she wanted everyone dead, she would have taken the life of anyone who fell into her domain.

Instead, she took them in, and made them great warriors. Just like she'll make me one, too. On the other hand, Maliu, his daughter and his wife sent us out here to be destroyed by these Shadow Flames. He even had a Wagiman name for it, so he has to be the one behind all this evil. Yep, Maliu is the evil person here. Now that I think about it, who today wears a loincloth? Not anyone I know.

204

Then there is Uli Marawara. That shaman probably isn't even related to us, and he gave us a vision. What human is capable of giving two schoolies a vision? He may even be the demon we're supposed to slay and he's twisted our thoughts to see Bastille as the villain. The snake. And we were gullible enough to fall for it!

Ira taps my shoulder again and motions for me to follow her. This time I do, without hesitating. We scale the course to a set of high ropes and she swings across them, while I take my time. Tires are my next challenge, and I find them easier than the ropes.

I follow her through each obstacle, and start to see the reason for this course. Accuracy is second to understanding the terrain and utilizing all aspects of it. You can have the greatest fighting strategy, but if your opponent knows a way to sneak around behind you without you seeing him, he has the upper hand. Well, I will have the upper hand over you Amber!

Ira takes me through a tunnel, leading out of the network. Blue patches peek through a cloudy sky. Red sandstone towers all around me. Before me, the Shadow Flames curl into the heavens. The only sound I hear is the soft drum roll of flames.

Walking out of the gully, I notice the Shadow Flames rage above the west side of the rock, too. Ira steps beside me, as I revel in the majesty of the flames.

We scale one of the rock faces to the top, and I know immediately my location. The vast desert plain of the Outback stretches before me. I am standing atop Australia's heart, the great, red sandstone known as Ayers Rock. I take a gander over the sloping edge. It is like standing outside the window of a thirty-story building.

I study the majesty of this rock. It is roughly two kilometers long, and just as wide, so a standard grocery store or the Sydney Opera House could fit twenty times across it. From where I stand, I can see that it resembles an arrowhead, with the side I just crawled up having a smoothed edge, as the opposing side resembles a serrated knife. The rock reflects a pinkish tinge in the midday sun.

The Shadow Flames are a fortress surrounding Ayers Rock, and from this ring, they scour the plain in all directions. One fissure heads for Alice Springs, branching off for

Darwin. Another runs eastward to Brisbane, Melbourne and everything in between. A third blazes a twisted path to Adelaide, and finally the west fissure heads for Perth. Beautiful chaos waiting to be unleashed. No more branching of the Shadow Flames, exactly as Maliu said, they remain stagnant and invisible to civilization. If Bastille wants to cleanse Australia, why is she waiting?

Distress and anxiety flood my arteries. Something in me demands an audience with Her Highness to find out the answer to this question. Abruptly, I leave Ira's side.

"Where're you going?"

"I want an audience with Her Greatness. Seeing this makes me wonder why she keeps the shadows stagnant."

"Oh no! Hold on there, mate. You cannot just waltz into Her Highness' chambers demanding an audience!"

"Why not?"

"Why not? Because, it just isn't done. Everyone knows you must be summoned to speak to her, and even then you must watch your tongue."

Her words dribble about my ear. I want an answer to this question, and the only way Ira is stopping me is standing outside my tunnel with her sword poised to clothesline me. I question Ira's loyalty to Bastille because she is trying to stop me from asking this.

I scale the face and head in through another tunnel. Ira trails me, warning me of the consequences to my decision, but a strong desire burns within me. It is similar to the way my sister gets when she's passionate about something. The answer to this question is of greater value to me than my life.

Suddenly, the passage narrows, and I have to shuffle through it with arms raised. Claustrophobia creeps up my spine, and I want to turn back. The tunnel walls kiss, forcing me to take a few steps back then crawl through the circular hole in the bottom of the crevasse.

In short order the squeeze opens into the main antechamber. I try to remember which tunnel leads to Bastille's chambers. The main tunnel before me probably leads to the obstacle course, so I try to imagine the network in my head, but the mental picture helps as much as a dry river does a thirsty man. I simply pick a tunnel, hoping it's the right one.

That is when Ira enters the antechamber, and realizes I *am* doing this. She points to a tunnel at an awkward angle to the floor. Right. The conversation with Hol rushes back to me. I rub my hands together and scale the wall into the hole.

Poking my head out of the hole, a man's angered voice nearly sends me down the chute.

"Who dare's enter Her Greatness' chamber without being summoned?"

A spear's tip pokes my head, and I look up to realize it's not a man speaking but a woman. Hol. I plead forgiveness, requesting to speak with Bastille about an urgent matter. Hol raises the spear, and helps me out of the hole. She instructs me to wait where I stand, while she heads into the room where the Spring of Rebirth is located.

Bastille emerges with Hol, a kind smile brightening her face. She beckons me to sit with her on the throne, so I join her. Bastille wraps her arm around me and asks me what is so urgent that I would risk death.

"Forgive me, Your Highness, I saw your magnificent Division Fire reaching its fingers to civilization, and I became concerned when I realized no one can see them. If you plan to cleanse Australia, why hide your creation?"

Bastille smiles beatifically, "You needn't concern yourself with them, Michael. All will be revealed in time. The New Order is approaching and gathering strength. When your sister arrives, you will be king over the city of your choice. For now, continue your journey with Ira."

I slide from her throne and bow to her as I step towards the hole. Bastille cautions me to watch my footing, so I turn sliding down the chute into the antechamber where Ira helps me to my feet.

"Well, you're alive, that's a relief. Was your question answered?"

I smile at her, and she buries her face in a hand. She says I remind her of a daughter she once had. The statement sparks an interest in me, so I ask. She waves her hands dismissively, and I realize she doesn't want to get into details. I imagine the memories are probably too painful to reminisce. Instead, she beckons me to the obstacle course. I run ahead of her and leap the gap to the sloping ledge. Scrambling up the slope, I hear her applaud behind me.

"Coo-aa! Coo-ee!" I call into the darkness.

"Coo-ee! Coo-aa!" Music to my ears.

I see someone wave a match in the air, and the torches light. I try the obstacles that gave me difficulty last time. The burning forest, particularly. I study the various paths. Last time I tried the forest floor path, so this time I decide the challenge of tree top path. The heat of the flames encourages me to move. I leap the last tree onto the gangplank and brush off soot and oil.

Next, I scale the waterfall, which simulates a torrential downpour or scaling a waterfall. The climb is difficult, as you can imagine, when water plunges right at your face and hands. My grip slips every time I reach for a new hold. Yet, as I struggle to grasp each nook in the wall, strength rises in me to press on, and try harder.

The next morning, I grudgingly rise before the sun. Ira tosses me a plate of berries and a naan, which is oven-baked flatbread. She orders me to get dressed and meet her atop Ayers Rock in five minutes. I fall back onto the straw. Five minutes! Flying squirrels are not even up at this unlawful hour, and she wants me to scramble through tunnels to meet her atop Ayers Rock in five minutes? What possesses this woman to get up so early anyway? I reckon it has something to do with my journey to becoming a warrior, but surely, it can wait until the afternoon.

I lay on the straw and close my eyes. A few more hours, I tell myself, or at least until seven.

"Get up you lazy sack o' meat! I want to be outside before the troops start beating the ground." It's Ira, and I assume she is talking about kangaroos, but I don't move. It's too early. Ira jabs me with a spear.

"Ow!" I say sitting up.

"Oh good, you're alive. Now get dressed!"

"Can I not have one more hour?"

"Oh, all right, but that's all I'm giving you so make the best of it."

I intend to.

The hour passes and I keep my end of the bargain. I get dressed, arm myself, and scramble through the tunnels of Uluru to the top of the rock. While grasping the sloping top of the rock to pull myself up, Ira nearly skewers me with the spear. The spear sails over my head and somewhere into the flames below.

"First rule of combat, mate: Mind your surroundings." She says as she helps me up. Then she slides down the rock to retrieve her spear while I lie down on the rock to catch a few more winks.

Ira returns and pokes me again with the spear. I stand, and she beckons me to attack her with my gauntlets. I hesitate. I don't want to hurt her, but she insists she will cope with whatever pain I deal to her, so I do, and she kicks me to the ground.

"I have battle scars like you wouldn't believe. Whatever you deal to me will be minor."

Thanks for the encouragement.

"Besides, if you wanna be a good fighter, don't rush someone head on." She lends me her hand. "Come at me again."

I try a different approach. I try running around to her back, but she extends the spear, knocking the wind out of me.

"Well, what are you waiting for? I said, come at me!"

I am *trying* to attack you, and I can see that head on isn't working.

I need to catch her off guard. Do something she will not expect. I rush her again. Then at the last possible second, I slide into her feet with my extended leg, and she loses her balance. She regains her footing smiling. I grin too. Ira urges me to try again.

As the sun rises, we switch roles. She takes the offense, so I have to block her. This part of the training is easier, but Ira is still relentless with her attacks, and it gives my mind a workout to anticipate her moves.

"You're improving faster than some," she says as she halts her attacks.

I smile. Amb, when we meet, I will show you how strong I have become. Then, after I have defeated you in a spar, we shall rule over Brisbane as royalty under our great Queen Bastille!

CHAPTER 7 I've Taught You All I Know

AMBER

"LEAN AGAINST THE WALL next time you climb up. You'll find it's easier to keep your grip on the wall." Desoto advises as I rub my rump from a fall.

I nod and try again.

I've practiced for a few weeks now, mastering everything Desoto has taught me, but this, concealing myself in the shadows while striking, I cannot seem to grasp. I'm either too visible or fall from my roost because the Gecko Blade slips. I would have given up long ago had it not been for my desire for Michael's return and a dedication to follow Yesh. These drive my spirit.

Alira also encourages me, telling me I'll get it eventually. She's supposed to be my opposition in these exercises. Desoto constantly reminds her to taunt me, which can be quite funny at times.

The suction head of an arrow sticks to the wall. "You don't have the guts Amb. You, " Alira breaks character peeling with laughter. I giggle too. It's good to know she is in high spirits again.

I cast a glance at Desoto. He is smiling and shaking his head. Alira draws her bow and fires at the target. Forgetting the climbing exercises for the moment, I launch a round as well from the wall. We both hit the target. Alira manages to hit the bulls-eye, and I am not far off. Desoto claps approvingly, and I cannot help beaming. We retrieve our ammunition.

"Let's try some one-to-one combat. Amber, remove your blades, but keep your gloves on. Alira catch." Desoto tosses her a sword.

Startled, I say. "Uh... Des, that's a real sword. Couldn't we start with training weapons or something?"

"That is a training weapon. It is dull enough that it will not kill you. A luxury I never had when I was under Bastille's thumb. With her it was learn the skill or die."

Desoto provides me tidbits of Bastille's character, and each bit only makes me despise her more. I long to rush into her domain and run her through, and before Yesh began guiding me, I would have done such an impulsive act.

What am I saying? I did do that! That's the reason I'm training here now. That's the reason Talo is dead. Amber you dork! Why did you have to drag Alira into this? All you had to do was go and get this training then her father would still be alive. This was your quest not hers.

Do not beat yourself up over your shortcomings, Amber. Though what you did was selfish and rash, you have come far since that day I spoke with you on the verge of the Shadow Flames.

Yesh speaks the truth. I *have* come a long way!

"Amber," says Desoto interrupting my thoughts. "Please to focus on the task at hand."

I apologize for zoning out. My face must have turned the color of a tomato, because Alira leans against the wall of the cave for support, laughing.

"As I was saying, this training is not for Alira, but for you." Desoto replies. I cast him a puzzled glance. "When you confronted Zietas, what was his primary weapon?"

You're going to make me think about this one. "He used a sword."

"Right, and what is Alira using?"

"A sword."

"Good. So what is the purpose of this exercise?"

"To learn how to confront someone with a sword?" I inquire.

"That is part of the answer..."

Part of the answer? What does he mean by part... oh! The light bulb glares. "It's to help me use my weapons better."

Desoto nods, and the smile that brightens my face must have filled the room. Desoto gives us the green light, but tells us to take our moves slowly listening to him. He instructs Alira to jab at me with the sword, and I instinctively duck out of the way.

"Stop," Desoto intervenes. "Amber return to the position before you avoided the jab of the training sword." I do. "Do you see a flaw to that stance?"

"Not really," I say craning my neck to look him in the face.

"Alira bring your sword down, please," he says. She does, and it touches my torso. I see what he means. "Had this been a real fight, you

218

would have been struck in a similar way. You have a weapon that is used as a long-range weapon. Take advantage of that. Keep out of reach, and when your opponent is exposed fire a round."

"But what about Zietas?"

"Zietas can wait. Right now, you need to focus on your technique and agility. Try again."

I nod.

In the hours that pass, I become better with my weapons. Then Desoto wrapped Alira's blade with rope and put suction cups on my blades so we could spar at regular speed. I avoid and jab, while taking a few blows from her sword.

Desoto steps between us, "Okay, I reckon you girls have done enough. Take a break, while I fetch some lunch."

We stop, and I take the time to wipe my brow. Alira stands next to me playing with her bowstring. I watch Desoto scramble over the rocks then turn my focus out across the gully savoring the cool breeze.

"Amb, your brother, what is he like?" Alira suddenly asks.

I blink, taken aback by the question. I know Michael better than anyone does, but no one has ever asked me to describe him. How do I respond to a question like that? I take a breath. To give her a simple answer like all right or analytical seems, well, childish. I want to paint my brother for her, let the traits I adore in him resound about the gully, but where do I start?

"Yakgarra! That's a difficult question. Where do I start?" I run my fingers through my hair chuckling. Then, I purse my lips.

"I didn't know you spoke Wagiman!"

"I know a little."

"Maman. That's good." She settled to her knees and said, "So tell me about your brother. Just start talking what you say will come."

"Well, all right. He's intelligent, got a great sense of humor. He likes to research *a lot*. A schmoozer. He's definitely a schmoozer, and I'm grateful for that because it keeps me from, well, nailing the blokes at Indro in the shin. Dependable. Courageous.

"When we were at the Shadow Flames, a perentie ambushed us and he..." tears well up in my eyes. "Excuse me," I raise a finger and wipe my eyes. "He pushed me out of the way, and took the fall for me."

"He sounds great!"

I smile nodding. Alira asks me what Michael looks like, so I do my best to describe him.

"He has red hair, darker than mine. Freckles dapple his face. Same eyes as mine. He has a spacer in his ear. He's taller than me, and fit."

By now, the tears trickle down my face. I wipe them away. Alira asks me if I want to stop, but I shake my head and continue. I tell her about moments when he made me laugh. That I envy his ability to go without studying for an exam, and still he manages to receive a seventy percent. I feel better talking about him. The conversation almost makes me feel as though he is beside me, playfully walloping my shoulder or cracking a joke. I still miss him, but this chat helps quench the fire of missing him, brings him closer, I guess.

Desoto returns with a Galah, and instructs Alira to make a fire. I offer to dress the bird, to which Desoto does not protest. I take the bird outside around the corner and dress it, carefully keeping my back to the flames. Removing the feathers and gizzards is easier this time than it was by the lake, but it still smells awful like, well, the bowels of a bird!

Desoto cooks the Galah, offering me a chance to turn it, but I decline. I would probably wind up burning our lunch, as I stare uselessly at the flames. Alira is a different case. She leaps at the invitation and marvels at the browning bird while I stare at the ceiling thumb wrestling.

When we sit down to lunch, Desoto takes the opportunity to educate us on how to enjoy a meal, and still be alert to our surroundings. He tells us to listen to everything, even in the midst of conversation, and instructs us always to have our weapons handy should the opposition strike.

Then he stands and walks out of the cave. I feel the cold tip of a sword against my neck, and hear Desoto telling me to try again to hear him. He walks back out encouraging Alira and me to talk, but I choose to listen for his footfalls. The soft scuff of his shoes on the stone gives him away and I use the Geckos to fend off his practice blade. Metal clashes, and I sweat enough to fill a pool, but I manage to point a clear shot at his gullet and he lets down his guard.

His smile brightens, showing all the approval I need. The weeks of practice have paid off. I've learned Desoto's fighting pattern, but I still have worries about confronting Zietas. One mistake and he'll run me through.

Let tomorrow worry about itself Amber, you have enough challenges for today.

Suddenly, Zietas bellows in the gully, his frustration of searching endlessly, evident. "Where are you Ambeeeeeer?!" His voice echoes about the gorge.

Alira and I freeze, but Desoto takes action. He orders us to scale the cliff and take refuge behind the bushes. We nod and begin the climb. I cast a dangerous glance into the gully. My bones seem to turn liquid, and I tremble.

Zietas stands atop the hill below us. His hands on hips and feet spread in an arrogant pose. I can envision the triumphant smile creasing his face. Panicking, I dive behind the bush. Alira scrambles after me. From our hiding place, I hear Zietas confront Desoto.

"Where is she, Desoto?"

"Who?"

"Don't toy with me, you traitor! I know she's here. I've spent days scouring every crevasse, tree, and hole of this blasted gully, only to stumble upon you. And what better way to announce your treason to Her Greatness than to teach the ankle-biter everything she taught you? I should run you through, but that can wait. I want the girl. Thanks to her little escapade, Her Greatness saw fit to gouge out my eye." He removes his hood, and I see the sunken, blood-crusted socket through the bramble.

So, Michael did not nick him. When I saw him out on the plain that was Bastille's doing. That explains his reduced depth perception, and why he shrouded his face under his hood.

Alira chunders. I cover her mouth. The pungent, chunky remnants of her lunch seep through my hand. I swallow my urge to follow suit, and wipe my hand on a patch of moss behind me.

"Allow me to explain the events that transpired after this incident." He pointed to his empty socket. "I ran into her a while back, and was about to carry her off, when by some ill-fate was knocked unconscious, and woke up with her gone. Before everything went black, I saw the man who threw the rock at me. So when I awoke, I found his house, but again she slipped through my fingers." He waggled a talon in front of Desoto's nose. "Now, look, here you are. So I'll ask you again. Where is Amber?"

"Bastille did you in again, did she? Caught you in another lie, huh?"

"Don't change the... what is that rank odor?"

"Oh, I just had lunch. Probably Galah gizzard."

I hear Zietas shuffle into the cavern. He smells Alira's regurgitated remnants of lunch, but he believes Desoto's fable.

I dare a peek at Desoto. We exchange glances and without mouthing words, he tells me to stay where I am. I acknowledge him. From where we are, we can see Zietas, but not the other way around. It is a perfect sleuthing point, until Alira sneezes. She reels back on the ledge, shaking the bush. Zietas briefly glances up, but turns to Desoto, and draws his sword. Talo flashes through my mind. I will not see another person die at the hand of this sociopath.

"Oy! Cyclops!" I stand, hollering to Zietas and revealing my position. "I'm the one you want, leave him alone."

Zietas whirls to face me, an evil smile curling his lips. I point my blades at him while he sheaths his sword and places his hands on his hips scoffing at my bravery.

"You are willing to try this again," he sneers with curling lips, "after what happened last time?"

"I've improved my skills since our first encounter."

"You have. I have no doubt in my mind that you have, however, my skill is still superior."

I slide down the cliff. Desoto instantly engages Zietas slashing from behind. Zietas defends himself with a dipping swirl of one sword, and at the same time attacks me with a second sword. He turns fully to face me, and though I'm able to block the swath of both swords, it's all I seem able to do. His attack is so fierce, he keeps me on the defense.

His fighting pattern is a blur as he aims for all my open spots. I side step and slash. Metal clashes as Zietas counters. Desoto and Alira join the battle, but even with three-on-one Zietas still has a supernatural advantage. His skill is otherworldly. Clashing or deflecting my blades into the gorge, he keeps Desoto at bay with his feet, and deflects Alira's arrows into the gully with his talons.

Then Zietas leaps off the cliff. We watch him plummet into the gully, his metal talons screeching and spraying four trails of sparks down the face of the cliff. I plunge gloved fingers into my ears, wincing. Zietas rolls and stands in the cleft, gazing up at us, flipping his swords. I prepare to jump, but Desoto cautions me.

"Hold up there, Amber, instead of just leaping to engage Zietas, ask yourself first why he would choose to continue this battle in the gully." I study the cleft, but do not see why Zietas would choose to fight in it.

"It's wider. He has more room to wield his swords. This strategy what you must grasp if you ever hope to have a chance at storming the Centipede's Nest.

"All this time, while Zietas engaged us he had been analyzing his surroundings. The gully, being wider than the cliff gives him more room to maneuver reaching the part of your body you cannot protect without armor, "

"My back." I finish.

"Right."

"Well, what do we do? We can't just let him stay there," my blades wobble, encompassing the gully, "he'll kill us in the night." I don't say it aloud, but I also want to retrieve the blades Zietas deflected into the gorge.

"True, Amber, he would." Desoto squeezed my shoulder, "I have taught you all I know, you and Alira are ready." He gave me a tiny push. "Take the bundle of blades next to my belongings, and make your way west to Uluru, I will do what I can to stall Zietas. Take the clothing with you. It will help you blend in with the locals."

I chuckle, and disappear into the cave. The Tree Leaper attire is with Desoto's belongings. He brought another pair knowing I would not take the first one he gave me. I change into the outfit (throwing on a pair of shorts under the skirt). The outfit reminds me of my Taekwondo uniform, since it allows me to move freely. I practice a jump-back-kick. I do another just because they're fun.

Alira enters the cave and wiggles into her attire, while I stuff the bundle of blades into my satchel. I glance at Alira. She's ready to go. I shoulder my pack. I stop Desoto from jumping into the gorge for a brief moment. He turns to me, a kind smile on his face.

I hug him. "Thanks for all you did for me. All you taught me."

His arms don't immediately wrap around me, so I reckon the situation is awkward for him. "A teacher can only be as good his pupils allow him to be, so thank you for being so willing to learn what I had to teach you."

I stand back, brushing a strand of hair behind my ear. My cheeks heat up, and we both know why, but he doesn't remind me of how we started, only how we finished. We finished strong, and I learned what I needed to from him, the rest was up to me (and Yesh, of course).

"Now take flight Amber, your wings are strong enough to leave the nest."

I nod, eyes welling slightly with tears smiling. Then I turn to Alira and we head off.

We sneak out a back way Desoto showed us during one of our lunch breaks. A tunnel connects our cave to a chamber with a pool. We weave around the pool and head toward a thin strip of light at the far end of this chamber where it opens out to another part of the gorge.

Then Zietas' words come to mind: *I've spent days scouring every crevasse of this accursed gully...* If he had checked everything he must have found this one too; maybe he did and moved on because it was only a mere slit in the wall.

I stuff my pack through the hole and worm my way through. Alira follows close behind. Miraculously, I see several of my blades glinting in the sunlight. In the distance, I can hear swords clashing. Good-bye, Desoto. Thank-you for all you've done for me. May Yesh give you the strength to vanquish Zietas.

CHAPTER 8 Infiltrate the Centipede's Nest

AMBER

NIGHT CHASES THE LAST RAYS OF SUNLIGHT into the shadows of Simpsons Gap. In the distance, I can see the Outback. The plain is orange and peaceful through the gully, while purple and orange clouds streak the sky. Normally, I would stop and take in the scene, but we are still a good day's walk away from Uluru, so I cannot stop. Zietas may be on our trail too, so I lengthen my strides. Alira yawns, stepping in stride with me. We walk in silence. I feel a storm brewing, and know that Bastille is stirring it.

I think about Michael. He must be sinking deeper into Bastille's grip. No, don't think that way Amb! Yesh will provide a way to save Michael. Focus on Bastille, and how to get into her domain.

Upon reaching the plain, we agree to stop for the night. The sun dips below the horizon, its last rays releasing the day. I lay on the ground gazing up at the stars. The day was long. I think about Desoto, and I ask Yesh to watch over him. I think of all the laughs we had together, and his method of training me. It was meek, but assertive, aggressive, but gentle. Part of me wants to practice the moves, the faints and lunges, and keeping to the shadows, but the other part, the stronger part, just wants to lie on the sand and rest, so I do.

My gaze turns to Alira. She's out like a light and sleeping soundlessly beside me. I turn back to the sky. A meteor streaks the heavens. It's light lasting a few seconds then vanishing. Silently amazed at what I saw, I continue to watch the stars until sleep finds me.

We arrive in Alice Springs a little after noon. I roll my cloak around my Geckos then stuff the bundle in my bag. I've never been one for fashion, but I know when something will stick out like a sore thumb! No sense in drawing undue attention.

Uluru is the local, indigenous term for Ayers Rock, I know that much, but where is it? I turn to Michael because he would know, only to realize he is not there to ask. Then I realize just how much I miss him. I turn the question on Alira and she simply shrugs.

"We're in Alice, may as well ask the locals. One of them is bound to know where Ayers Rock is." Her suggestion is worth a try.

The first person we come across is a husky man tinkering with his bike. He wears a black muscle shirt, blue shorts, and running shoes. His back is to us so all I can see is his graying ponytail with black streaks. I throw my hair back with a band, and put on an inquiring expression.

"Excuse me, sir?" I ask walking up to the man. He stops tightening a nut, and turns his head to us. His initial scowl melts into a smile, which I find a tad unsettling. I force myself not to back up, but stand erect. I reckon he notices my nervousness anyways.

"Can I help you sheilas?" His voice is gruff and soft all at once.

I find my voice and skip the introductions. "We lost our guide, and we're wondering if you could point us to Ayers Rock." The lie chokes my throat, and the man notices.

"Strange reports have been coming from that neck of the bush lately. Heard talk of ghostly thylacine yowling in the twilight hours, and perentie the size of children roaming the plain. I don't believe it myself, but it's got most of Alice spooked. Some even claim to have seen these creatures for themselves, so just in case there is something going on 'round here I'd stay clear of that place."

I sigh, brushing a stray lock behind my ear. Useful information, but they still don't tell me where the rock is or how to reach it, so I decide to resort to the truth. "What if I told you everything you just said was real? What if I told you there was a wall of black fires raging just outside of your town waiting to engulf it? Would you point us in the direction of Ayers Rock then?"

"I'd say you're dehydrated and delusional from walking in the sun too long, but I can point you in the direction of The Rock. It's six hours southwest of here. Why are you so keen on going there anyway?"

"Call me bananas, but my great grandfather gave me a vision a few weeks ago, and well, it sort of depicted the end of the world. Everything you just described to me is only small contractions. Things will only get worse if my brother and I do not stop the demon behind all this evil."

The man's jaw drops, and he stares at me. His expression crumples, and then he roars with laughter. "You spin quite a yarn sheila!" He shakes his wrench in my face still laughing.

"Your grandfather giving you a vision about the end of the world? That's a good one! Did your grandfather have a didge, eat locusts and wear tribal paint?"

"It's Amber. And I don't know. Also, I don't appreciate you mocking me. You can believe what I say or not, but don't insult me.

"Besides, I've seen things that would make your skin crawl. I'm out here because my brother was dragged into a wall of black flames by the very lizard you just described. When I went in after him, I discovered a shadow of my brother who tried to kill me. Later, a follower of this demon, with metal talons on his right hand and a hood pulled over his face, brought me to Death's doorstep. I saw him again just yesterday in Simpsons Gap, "

The man returns to his bike shaking his head and muttering to himself. He isn't going to help us any further, so I beckon Alira to follow me. The man's voice stops us. "You're not thinking of heading to The Rock on foot are you? When I said six hours I meant by car."

"How long on foot?" I ask.

He casts a calculating gander over us and says, "Given your physique I'd say five days at least."

I place my hands on my hips, and ask, "What do you mean by that?" Although, I'm actually pretty sure I know where he is going with it.

He shrugs, "Well, maybe four if you walk quickly, but do you really want to go there with the knowledge you have. Would it not be easier to go home and forget the whole thing?"

"It would be easier to buy a ticket and take a train back to Brisbane, but that would mean leaving my brother in the hands of a power-mongering demon. It also means failing to complete the mission my grandfather gave to me. That is something I refuse to do. Like I said before, I'm here because I choose to be."

The man returns to his bike. He takes his wrench to a nut and tightens it. Looks like I'm walking. Besides, I have the information I need, so there's no point in sticking around. I start to walk away. Alira follows.

"Wait," he says. Mid-step, I pivot. He is heaving himself up. "I am going out with a couple of friends for a joy ride. You are welcome to tag along in the sidecar. It's in my garage."

I thank him for his generosity. I'll reach Uluru by night fall! Walking into his garage, I see it leaning on the back wall. I rub my hands together then attempt to wheel it out. The sidecar is heavier than it looks. Alira must have seen my struggles because she lends a hand. We manage to take it to the door, and from there the man takes over. In short order it's attached to his bike.

"There is an extra helmet hanging on the wall, you're welcome to it if you like." I give the helmet to Alira, and take the sidecar.

"I wanted the chair, though," she whines.

"All right, give me the helmet and I'll give you the sidecar."

She hesitates. "Why do you need the helmet?"

The man answers her as he swings a leg over the bike's seat, "Because the side car is safer than sitting behind me, that's why." I raise an eyebrow. Alira gives up the helmet and hops into the sidecar.

Motorcycles sputter up the street. Alira and I watch the group pull up to the house, and I can feel their rumbling in my bones.

"How ya goin' Damian?" The man asks the one who steps off his bike first.

"Ready to kick up a dust cloud and rattle the desert," Damian replies. The bloke's gaze turns to us. "Your nieces gonna tag along, Greg?"

"Holy dooley! You have nieces? Since when?" pipes up another.

"Naw, they're not mob. Just a couple o' tabbies lookin' for a ride to The Rock."

Damian takes Greg aside, and I can guess what they are discussing. I remove the helmet and step from the bike, pointing to my bag. Alira points at the bag too, and I nod, so she hands it to me. I shoulder it, as the two men walk back over to us. Damian gets on his bike. Greg looks at me, his eyebrows raise silently questioning why I'm carrying my bag.

"I said I'd drive you two ladies to The Rock, didn't I?"

"Yes, but I reckon you, "

"Changed my mind? Why would I do that?"

I have no answer, because I based my actions on stereotypes, which now I feel horrible about doing. When Greg walked out of earshot with Damian, I immediately thought Damian was pointing out the wrench Alira and I was throwing into their plans. I thought they probably thought going to Uluru was out of the way from their route. I apologize to Greg for being so judgmental.

"No worries. Frankly, Damian doesn't care where we go. He's just looking for some good times on the road, but he's skeptical about The Rock, so I told him we'll turn around at the Red Centre Way."

"Greg, quit yabbering and let's go, mate. I want to get at least to Darwin before the sun sets."

We say good-bye to Greg and his gang and part our ways. They turn around and we head to Uluru. When the rumble of their motors is far enough away, I throw on my cloak and arm myself, while Alira changes.

In a few minutes, Alira and I journey west according to her instructions. I glance around.

The Shadow Flames of Uluru

Shadow Flames stretch to my right and left. I take a swig of the stale water in my canteen, and then rub my eyes. Both branches of the Shadow Flames remain.

Abruptly, a screaming headache drops me to my knees. Alira is at my side, her words just a murmur in my ears. I feel her hand on my shoulder.

Color fades to a blurry mash of black and white. The green shrub and reddish soil before me mingle into a single blob. Then, I see Uluru encircled by raging Shadow Flames like a fiery fortress. Shadow Flames spread from the Red Heart like a plague towards the coastlines of Australia. Now geography was never my strongest subject, but I know enough about my country to know most of the population lives along the coastline.

Somehow, I understand what I am seeing is a premonition of things to come. It continues, and I see Michael as if he is standing in front of me. He stands atop Uluru overlooking the Shadow Flames. He wears the garb of a Tree Leaper, his gauntlets loaded and at his sides. A green, hooded cloak covers his shoulders and the trousers he wears are tarnished. His feet are bare, scarred and bruised. And he wears no top showing off his new six-pack and pectorals to the world, his eyes are madly searching the plain for something. A way out? Me? Then we lock eyes, and a surly smile creases his lips.

"Amber!" Alira shakes my shoulders. I stand abruptly and dizziness sets in. Alira steadies me.

"C'mon, we don't have much time." I try to take off running. Alira grips my arm, so I slow to a walk.

"You stared into space like you were seeing a ghost."

"I saw Michael again." I say. "This time he was standing on Uluru gazing out across the plain. We locked eyes for a second, and I could see pain on his face. And," I paused, unsure of it at first, "yes, anger, too. There was anger, too."

Alira tells me it was only an episode similar to what I had back in Simpsons Gap, and I want to believe her, but I cannot help wondering if I am actually connecting with him.

He once told me that some twins have this special connection. They share similar thoughts, pain, and the like. I remember challenging the theory, now I'm having second guesses. Could we actually be able to sense each other across vast distances? It'd be awesome if that were the case! To know where he is, what he's doing... maybe it's not all that great now that I think about it. Still, I saw his pain, and I have to get to him. I need to get to him.

I continue walking west, looking over my shoulder to encourage Alira to keep up. She jogs up to me, asking if I'm all right. The premonition has passed. I reckon I will be fine, and hopefully, I will not have another one.

Uluru looms on the horizon. I decide to hide my bag in the hollow of a Eucalyptus. Time to raid the nest, I muse smiling at the thought of surprising Bastille. As I near Australia's great red heart, the presence of evil grows. The thylacine skull flashes in my mind. I quicken my pace, only to stop at the wall of Shadow Flames that encroach Uluru.

It is exactly like my premonition. The flames tear across the land in all directions from this ring. The fires breathe and growl, emitting the same draft I felt before. I load my gauntlets, but detach the chains, so I won't shoot Alira in the leg. Then I grasp her hand, and we exchange looks of nervousness. She nods. I manage a shaky breath. *Banzai*. We charge the fires.

The frigid air within the fires hits me like a wall of ice once again, and Alira's grip tightens. I cope with the pain, because the thought of losing her in here is worse than the pressure of her hand.

The fires roil and swirl around us. With each step, the urge to turn around and give up is heavy, like a water balloon sagging from the tap threatening to burst. My legs are lead, and the Geckos weigh on my shoulders. The thylacine's skull dances in front of me with a petrified, grinning maw. I am not deterred because I have to press on. Michael's freedom drives my heart and spurs my longing to get through this hellish shadow. Even my doppelganger forming before me doesn't turn me away. I slash at her and she vanishes.

Suddenly, my hand touches rock, and I look up. Flames shroud an azure sky. We are losing daylight, so I turn to Alira, asking for any information on Uluru. I know it's a rock made of sandstone, but that's it. I reckon, since she grew up out here she might know a little more than I do.

"Uluru is a sacred rock to our people, "

She said, *our people*, so she's referring to me as well?

", our ancestors used to come to the caves within Uluru to seek refuge, to tell others of legends, or to pray. I reckon, Bastille is poisoning the land from these caves."

Caves. Okay, I'll buy that. Where better to hide from the world while you plot to destroy it than inside a cave? Come to think of it (and I'm playing analyst again) it's the perfect hideout. It's a giant rock, and a Wonder of the World, I think that is perfect protection. No one would think to explode it, even if they knew a demon resided inside it. The rest of the world would be up in arms if anything besides a natural disaster harmed it. It's isolated. It's at the heart of Australia! It's perfect, and devious, I might add, and a tad cowardly.

From the air, Ayers Rock looks like a deformed foot with the toes facing southwest. At least I believe that is how my geography teacher described it in ninth grade.

Loading my Geckos, I decide to start with the cave that has the strongest presence of evil. I find it wedged between two of Uluru's toes.

We descend into the tunnel. A long passage narrows to a crevasse. I shuffle through it, pressing my back against one wall, only to get stuck halfway.

Alira crawls through the tunnel to my feet where she stops and looks up at me smiling. I blow at a tassel of hair. Leave it to me, to find the hardest way.

We back up, and then I crawl through on my hands and knees. Alira and I worm our way through the tight squeeze, until the evil is stronger than ever, and my limbs feel almost like jelly. I'm coming Michael! Just hang on, little brother.

Finally able to stand again, we look around a large antechamber littered with tunnels. Tunnels before us, tunnels beside and behind us, and tunnels above us at different angles. The place reminds me of Swiss cheese. I give up counting after twenty.

The place reeks of evil. But what I find interesting about every tunnel is that each is almost a perfect circle, and I wonder what could make such a passage?

I think I'll probably find the answer to that question later, so I let the thought slip from my mind. Then it occurs to me. Where is everyone? There should be someone standing guard, right?

I take a step into the antechamber. No traps like a cage falling from the ceiling spring. No one lunges from the shadows. The place is deserted? Why?

"You think we found the wrong cave?" Alira whispers.

"No, this is the place. I haven't felt this jittery since Zietas attacked us in Simpsons Gap. Besides, if it wasn't, I'm sure Yesh would have told me."

Suddenly, another vision sends my head spinning. I lean against the cavern wall to steady myself. In this vision, I see a masked man about my brother's height standing on a sloping rock with a wall of everyday fire burning behind him. Surrounding him are pieces of wood dangling on ropes, rope bridges and nets and high ropes. His physique reminds me of someone I saw once. Perhaps one of the Tree Leapers who ambushed us in the clearing, but he's wearing a pair of gauntlets similar to Michael's. Before I can figure out who the person is, the vision ends. I press my palm against my forehead. There must be a reason for these events. Perhaps Yesh will know, so I ask.

I do not need to tell you what you already know, He replies.

What I already know? I don't know why I keep having these visions. Even if I do know, I want an answer. Surely, that's a good enough reason.

What you want, Amber, is to talk, which I am never opposed to doing. However, I think you should focus on the task.

He has a point. Now is not the time to ask about these premonitions (though I'm dying to know), now is the time to vanquish Bastille and get my brother back!

A gut feeling rises within me to pick the center tunnel, so I charge the tunnel. It ends at a cliff. My legs flail through the air, propelling me, well it feels like that, towards a sloping ledge, on which I land flat on my stomach. The blow winds me. Behind me, I hear a splash, followed by Alira's shock from hitting the water. She swims over to the ledge, and climbs up.

"Coo-aa! Coo-ee!" a voice crows in the darkness.

"Coo-ee! Coo-aa!" comes a reply.

The cavern lights up, as I stand in awe at the obstacle course. My eyes fall on a figure standing in front of a wall of fire. I attach the chains to the thumbs of my gauntlets.

"Oy!" I call to the figure. "Have you seen a red-haired bloke about this pit?" The figure turns to face me from the fire, and I recognize the voice instantly.

"I'm hurt Amb. You don't recognize your own twin?"

CHAPTER 9 Come To Your Senses!

MICHAEL

MY SISTER'S FACE LIGHTS UP when she sees me, but that smile is brief, so I try to lighten her spirits.

"How ya goin', Amb? I missed you, ya know?"

"I know. I missed you too."

"Well, we're together again, there's no need to worry anymore."

Amber stares at the floor. Why is she not happy to see me? She should be overjoyed. Maybe she is and she is just trying to hide her emotions as usual. Then again, she always has been able to read me better than I could her, so perhaps she is happy to see me and I'm misinterpreting her emotion as melancholy. I decide to probe.

"You seem distant Amb, why?"

"It's just that I really missed you." She already established that, and I understood it the first time, so why is she saying it again. I wait for her explanation, which never comes.

Perhaps a spar might get her talking, and might span the chasm between us. With that in mind, I load my knives, but to my confusion, she simply removes hers. What is with her today? She used to get fired up about sparring. I used to connect with her! Why is she so distant? Something happened to her, maybe she blames herself for losing me at the Shadow Flames, and she should. After all it was her fault. Bastille said so. Not to mention, she engaged the perentie when she should have just let it alone.

My emotions hit rapids, and I point my blades at her, but she does not budge. She just curls her hair with a finger, looking at me with sadness in her eyes.

"Do something Amb! Side step, talk to me, anything!" She does not move. "Come on Amber!" I close the gap between us and poke her with the tip of my blade drawing blood, and she puts a hand over the nick as a tear trickles out of her eye. "Fight me, you dag! What are you waiting for?"

She shakes her head. "I will not spar with you Mike, not while you're lost."

Lost? I'm not lost. I know exactly where I am. Maybe *she* is lost. Lost a few marbles, that's what. Then again, she could be tired, so I offer her my room to sleep, and in the morning she can meet Bastille. Then she'll see that she isn't what Uli and Maliu said she was. Perhaps she would be interested in seeing the Shadow Flames from the crest of Ayers Rock, so she can see the grandeur of them. Then she'll see that Bastille is using them to create a new world, one without suffering or pain. A world where everyone will live together in peace under the Centipede.

I turn and head for the exit to the top of the Rock, but Amber does not follow. When I look back, she is sitting on the sloping start of the obstacle course with her head buried in her hands. The other girl is kneeling beside her, and appears to be consoling her. I don't yet know her name, but I do find her attractive. Amber looks to the roof of the cave her eyes wet with tears. I cannot think of the last time when my sister cried. Something is wrong.

I walk over and kneel in front of her, but she doesn't take notice, so I wave my hand in her face. The girl scowls at me.

"This is your brother? He is not acting very considerate to you."

"Yes, he is my brother and that is what grieves me."

137

"Hold it you're grieving because you're related to me? What in heaven's name has gotten into you, Amb? Tell me now, or I'm taking you to see Bastille!"

Amber stands and starts to walk away from me, so I grab her wrist, and she tries to wrench free, but I hold my grip. She may be better at sparring, but I'm still stronger, so I use that strength to pull her back toward me and wrap my arms around her.

I want to get into her head, to know what she is thinking, so I hold her in a hug. She only pushes free of my arms. "What's with you, Amber? Tell me, please." I struggle to contain my discontent at her melancholy manner.

Her expression remains glum. I grab her by the hand. This time she allows me to take it. We are going to see Bastille, because I want answers. Bastille said my sister would be glad to see me, yet when we finally meet, she is distraught and grieving about being related to me? I don't know why, but Bastille will.

I half drag her through the tunnels, while her resistance to follow is evident. Behind us trails that other girl. I could walk through these tunnels in two minutes, but with Amber giving resistance it takes longer. I wish she would just tell me what she is feeling, but she refuses to speak to me. I begin to wonder if she is sorry for being my twin. If that is the case, she cannot change that. She can hate me, grieve for me, whatever she wants to do, but we are *blood*, and nothing changes that. If she has decided to be my enemy, then I will have to accept that, too.

When we finally, enter the back tunnel leading to Bastille's chambers, Lepez greets me warmly, but frowns at Amber and the other girl. I tell him they are with me, and that they would like to see Bastille. He walks down the tunnel to her chamber, and returns within a minute to beckon us in with a bow. Bastille sits on her throne when we enter a smile creasing her face. I bow, but Amber and the other girl do not. Bastille raises her head in anger at the defiance.

"Forgive me, Your Majesty, but my sister does not realize that you demand respect by all." I cast a glower at her, but she does not change her stance of opposition. I turn her to face me. "Amb, show some respect will you?" I whisper.

"Mike, I won't give this demon the satisfaction of my submission, even if it is just a facade." She looks straight into Bastille's eyes. A sign she considers Bastille as her equal! Bastille rises from her throne, placing her hand in the fold of her robe. The thought of losing her terrifies me.

"Your Majesty, please reconsider! My sister does not know who you are. She just needs time to warm up to you. She is stubborn that way. Take me in her place to quell your wrath, but spare her life! I beg you!"

"No Michael, your sister has made her decision. Therefore, since your sister doesn't wish to join us then she will not be a part of the New World. In fact, you should be the one to do the execution. Slay your sister now, before me, so that I know you truly wish to follow me."

I hesitate. Bastille promised that Amber would join me. She *promised* that we would rule over Brisbane *together* in the New World, but Amber just shattered this dream. She is steadfast in her ways (as usual), and I know nothing will make her change them. Perhaps the Spring of Rebirth would help her see. I have to try it or I lose my twin forever.

"Your Greatness? What about the Spring of Rebirth, could Amber see it? Perhaps if she saw it, she would appreciate your cause."

My gaze turns to my sister for approval, only to see her shake her head, so I take her aside, out of Bastille's earshot. "Amber what is with you, I'm trying to save you from death here."

"Michael I would rather die than join that witch. Desoto was under her grip, and he sought a way out, so no. I will not join her."

Bastille beckons me, "What is ailing you, Michael? Your hesitation is disturbing. Do you wish to follow me or die with your sister? The choice is yours, but you better make it soon, because my patience is wearing thin."

Hand still in the fold of her robe, Bastille's eyes blaze with anger. What is even more terrifying is her quiet, dulcet tone. It is almost as if the anger gives her pleasure. I have never heard this kind of anger before, nor have I seen this side of Bastille. The Bastille I know is kind and loving.

This Bastille is insidiously sadistic and evil. I want to keep my life, but I also cannot bring myself to slay my sister, at least not after

Bastille promised we would be together. My arm raises and I poise my blades for her heart. Amber closes her eyes, and I see a tear trickle from her eye. The girl aims her bow, so if I shoot Amber she will loose an arrow at me. Then Bastille will probably take the girl's life, so in the end all three of us die. And Bastille loses two assets.

But I cannot bring myself to fire at my sister. Without her, I am incomplete, because only she can fill that void in my life. Perhaps, in time, the wound might heal, though not without leaving a scar.

"Come to your senses, mate!" the girl suddenly blurts out. "That witch is using you! She has never cared for you. Whatever she promised you will never come to pass. Desoto said so."

I blink. What spurs such an outburst? For that matter, what does she know about Bastille? Then something cracks loose, and I feel as though she just plucked scales from my eyes.

I turn to face Bastille. Her emerald eyes burn with malice and abhorrence, and I can see in them the quiet rage against me and the treason I considered.

For the first time, I begin to question if Her Majesty is everything I thought her to be. The once kind and consoling woman I knew, now skewers me with eyes of death. Everything fades into the background. All sound ceases. The only two people in this room right now are her and me. Her gaze is steadfast, unblinking. She is a statue with a piercing gaze that burns into my very core.

"Michael, do not keep me waiting!" Bastille growls, and I see a segmented leg emerge from the fold in her robe.

I drop my blades. Even if Amber is my enemy, I cannot execute her.

Well, actually if I do it, she would haunt me every night. In my dreams, she would always be in the shadows, or in a crowd. She would be wearing this sad, pleading expression every time, and though I would tell her to go away, I know I could never bring myself to rid myself of her. As I said before she has a place in my heart, and if I take her life, I may as well carve a hole in my heart too.

Bastille's face smolders in rage. She presses her fingers together and rests them against her mouth. Then, with her eyes still fixed on me, she rises from her throne removing a stick from the fold in her robe. The stick turns out to be a multi-jointed leg, which she flexes straight. I back towards the hole leading to the antechamber. I remember seeing that leg. She used it to gouge out someone's eye when he lied to her! Now she is threatening to use it on me!

I do not want Amber to see me eat my eye, or hers. Then Amber steps in front of me. Even after all I've done, she still cares for my wellbeing. Once again, she is taking a stand for me. Heat flashes through me.

A rage against my sister boils within me, and I act. I push her to the ground, and force her backwards aiming my blades at her. I cast a gander at Bastille, who has stopped to see what I will do. Turning back to my sister, I see the fear in her eyes, but it does not deter me this time. I'm tired of being her inferior! It's time I show her that I am stronger!

"Michael, what is this about, I was trying to save you!" The tears roll down her face. I kick her shin still scowling at her. "Michael, stop!" But I do not stop. The power I have over her intoxicates me, filling my thoughts.

Her words plague my ego like a cancer. "That's exactly why I'm doing this! I'm done playing second fiddle to you, Amber! You've always been better in combat than me, and I'm going to change that!" I lunge for her, and she blocks me with her gauntlets, but I land atop her, and put my blade at her throat.

Amber closes her eyes, but the tears still flood her face. I haul her to her feet and kick her to the ground again, ordering her to fight me. Yet she takes every blow and every slash until she falls face down at my feet, and grabs hold of her wounds sobbing, "Why, Michael?"

Is she deaf? I told her why! Did she not hear what I said? "I will not be second best!" My sister lies on the floor, her cedar hair shrouding her face, and she holds her stomach. Then she looks at me, her hair conceals one eye. I turn my back, disowning her as my twin.

"Do what you want with her Bastille. I'm done here. As you said, if she is not with us then she is against us." I begin to walk towards the hole when my sister speaks.

"Michael..." she manages through sobs from grief and the wounds I inflicted on her. "Look inside yourself. Wherever that lie came from, that is what it is. A lie. There are lots of things you do better than me."

"Name one."

"You're better at talking with people than I am. Our first year at Indro, you made friends the first day, whereas it took a week for me to make friends. You are able to present reasonable cases for the theories that you figure out. Like how you discovered the pack of thylacine we faced had no visual impairment. That's something I wish I could do. And how you can walk into an exam without studying a single minute prior and yet you still earn a B. You're more intelligent that I am, Mike. You always have been, and I envy that about you."

I turn around, as Bastille's words echo in my head. *You already know you are smarter than she is, and she knows it too, but she will never openly admit this to you. She has too much pride... too much pride...* And yet here she is admitting to me that I am smarter than her!

"And when we were in that clearing next to the Shadow Flames, you saved me from that perentie."

"If by saving you means getting myself caught and dragged into the Shadow Flames, then yes, I saved you. And yet, I must thank-you for engaging that beast, because I would have never realized how much you use me. How much you push me around. You know it's funny how, when we're opposing each other, I finally see your true colors, Amb, and you treat me no better than the blokes at Indro."

"Michael, that's raw prawn! The blokes at Indro have nothing to do with how I treat my blood, and not just blood, but my other half. How I treat your *gender*, if I understand you correctly, is different than how I treat you as a person. I can treat a man on the street like dirt, but I will never do that to you. I can break the hearts of every immature, wannabe-boyfriend at Indro, but you are my twin! That relationship is not the same! I will always love you Michael. Always."

I pause. She will never understand, and how can she? Still, I reckon I can try my best to explain myself to her.

"Actually Amber, how you treat one man is how you treat *all* men, and just in case you forgot, I'm a man! So you treat me the same way, or maybe you do treat me slightly better, I've never really analyzed that. Oh, wait, yes! That day when you confronted Travis and you snapped at me making me feel like an idiot? Remember that? Of course you do. I mean, why wouldn't you? How did you put it? Ah, yes, you said, 'of course not! He would think I have kangaroos loose in the top paddock' You may as well have called me an idiot to my face! Look me in the eye and tell me that is not an example of treating me the same way you treated Travis."

She looks me in the eye, but her hair still covers one. "Michael, you're right. I did snap at you that day, and I was wrong in turning my frustration towards Travis upon you, but I never meant to hurt you."

"Whatever, so saying I did save you from that Komodo, perentie, or whatever it was, one occurrence will not make up for nine years of 'better luck next time, mate', or 'av-a-go-ya-mug' and 'you'll eventually pin her'. You're not a man, so you can't know what those responses do my reputation. I'm fifteen and my sister still has better technique than me. That starts to erode at my image, despite my efforts to conceal it."

"It erodes because you let it, Mike, and if this is about Taekwondo, you *are* good. There are countless in our belt level you can knock to the ground, and you are stronger than me, you just proved it on the obstacle course, when you held my wrist, or when Dad needs help lifting heavy objects he calls on *you*. Mum and I will get in there to help if it's *really* heavy, but most of the time you and Dad have it under control!" She smiles, trying to make light of the situation. "Not only that, but you manage to pull off feats with your, for lack of a better word, handicap that I only wish I can do! When you land wrong, you limp, but you still insist on continuing despite Instructor Seung's suggestions to rest. And for the record, I'm no better at the techniques, then you are; I'm just squeamish and guard myself more, getting in where I can."

"Exactly. You're better, because you can do that. Well, guess what Amb, now it's my turn! Now I'm superior to you. Now you're the one who's on the ground in humiliation!"

"No, Michael, I'm here because I'm grieving, and I'm grieving because you believe glory and self-satisfaction is more important than my life."

I fire a blade ripping her attire and grazing her arm, but it only makes her tears flow all the more. Then she lies on her arm, and I see something in her that I had lost sight of, something from our distant past when we were

137

but ankle-biters laughing and always joyous in each other's company.

I see my fraternal sister, the one I loved and cared about under the monkey bars lying on an arm twisted behind her, and I see myself leaping from the slide and running to her aid. In the car to the hospital, I am consoling her and holding her arm.

A tiny spark in my heart flickers to life. That flame that always rekindled after the worst of our squabbles burns hot, and melts the ice.

"Time's up Michael!" Bastille muses. "And it looks like you've made your decision. Hol?" Hol pokes her head in the archway. "Take these three to the lower tunnels and leave them there to rot while I decide a suitable execution for this treason!"

CHAPTER 10 Past on a Wall

MICHAEL

BANDAGING THE WOUNDS I INFLICTED on Amber rips a few emotional ones in my heart. The lower tunnels are dank and dark. Hol did leave us one little candle, so I'm bandaging more by feel than by sight. That doesn't stop my mouth, though. I continually apologize to her for injuring her. She tells me I wasn't myself. I know that now. Still, I despise myself for allowing Bastille to bend my will so easily. Me. The bookworm. The brainyac who researches for a passed time was suckered into believing a lie! A lie about my sister that I should have easily deflected.

"Michael," my sister consoles, touching my face, "you succumbed to Bastille because she brought to the surface a desire you suppressed for years. You longed to surpass me in combative skills because you were tired of the criticism you received from others, and though they meant well, you said it wore on your image. That kind of thing can deflate the best self-confidence."

I vaguely remember saying this, and I guess it goes to show that words do seep into a person's subconscious despite their efforts to ignore them. That said, everything I told my sister in that state of mind, she must recall vividly, so I ask her what else I said to her, but she shakes her head, probably to spare me further grief. However, she does ask me if I recollect communicating with her across vast distances.

I'm confused, and my expression tells her so. I have no idea what she is talking about. Thankfully, she sees my confusion, even in this dull light, and explains herself. She says she saw me standing atop Uluru, gazing out across the plain, which disturbs and intrigues me. The disturbing part is the Shadow Flames stretching for every inch of civilization, but what peaks my interest is her ability to see me in her vision of that plain.

"How does it work?" I ask.

"I dunno, it just sort of happens, but you once told me that some twins could communicate with each other. They had this special connection that when one feels pain the other one does too, or something like that." She tries to sit up, so I help her.

Perhaps I saw that philosophy in a movie or read it somewhere, because I do not recall telling her that, although it would be amazing to possess such a talent, I could live without the pain aspect of it, however. That could be a hindrance in combat, Taekwondo even, and I'm sure it would look bizarre to others watching if I jabbed her in the arm then held mine in pain.

Amber says she also saw me when I jumped into the pool. Now I *really* want answers. How did she know? Then I remember seeing a ghost pounding on the crystalline wall. No. That could not have been her. Could it? I ask her to explain. Then I connect the dots.

She dreamed she saw me jumping into the pool, and in that dream when I saw the splatter of blood, she actually bloodied her knuckles on the floor of a cave where she was staying. The line of dots suddenly stops. I saw her in the pool though. So how could she be in two places at once? Like a fingerprint on a piece of paper flashes to life under a black light, I realize that wasn't my sister in the pool.

That was Bastille tainting my thoughts. From the very beginning of our quest she had been working on me. That pool was my make or break point, and I broke. I gave into the lie that I needed to be better than my sister in every aspect of my life. Now I hate myself for that weakness and that, well, how should I put it?

I cuss aloud and jump to my feet. I have trouble dealing with these emotions, so I pace the chamber. I have to face it. I lost any good sense I possessed, and traded it for the lie. What a dimwit.

The other girl touches my shoulder. I look into her eyes. They crinkle at the corners, and I find a sense of peace in their smile.

"The dark time is over Michael. Let go," she says. I nod.

Then I remember my manners. "I don't believe we've been properly introduced. You know my name through the grapevine, but I don't know yours."

"Yes, Amb told me your name. My name is Alira, but your sister calls me Ali. You can, too, if you like."

"It's a pretty name," I say. I reckon she is blushing because she looks shyly at the ground. Her hands are behind her back, and she's swaying. She really is kinda cute.

I want to have a conversation with her, get to know her, but we have a continent (and maybe the world) to save. Clearing my throat, I turn my attention to my sister, and I ask if she is all right. She shrugs, which is good enough for me. Now we need a plan to escape.

"Michael the place is crawling with Tree Leapers. It is going to be difficult getting out of here without being seen."

"They're not the problem."

"What do you mean they're not the problem? Of course they're a problem!"

"Believe me Amb, they're clueless about us. The only two we'd have to worry about are Hol and Zietas. I remember Ira telling me that Bastille does not hold a ceremony for new recruits, so we can use this to our advantage by passing off as new recruits. It will work."

"In theory. Don't forget you're a traitor now. I reckon that news will get around."

"Do I detect an analytical mindset? That's my job isn't it?"

She smiles, "I had to keep you alive in my thoughts somehow, didn't I?"

"That is a good way to go about it," I reply.

"Anyway," my sister continues, "as I was saying, Desoto is considered a traitor here, too. I'll put money on it that if he were to walk in here right now, he'd be executed."

"Hold it. Desoto, the coward who wanted to see you face a thylacine, is now a traitor? Since when?"

"Long-story short, he joined Bastille because she promised him courage. He soon found out that she never really helped him, but made him more afraid. So, while still managing to keep up a façade, he began to seek other means to find courage. Then he just up and left one day and never looked back."

"How do you know this? Did you meet him on the road to Ayers Rock or something?"

"Actually, I was told by Yesh to head to Simpsons Gap to train before I came to rescue you."

My interest is sharpened by her casual mention of this Yesh person. I want to know more. "Who is Yesh?"

"How do I put this?" Amb pauses in thought. "He's like a mentor, guiding you in what's right. I reckon he knew I would need training before I went to Ayers Rock, so he told me to do it, sort of like how Jonah was told to go to Nineveh."

I purse my lips nodding, completely intrigued.

"A day's walk into my journey towards The Red Center, because I'm stubborn that way, Zietas shows up." She grins at me, "let's just say he made my fighting tactics look like a tap on the shoulder."

My eyes widen, as I laugh through my nose.

"Yeah, it was a bit of a wakeup call after being unconscious for three days." She moves her hands with palms up like a scale illustrating her allusion. "Jonah in the fish for three days, me on a bed unconscious, similar story. Then, Zietas shows up and burns the house I was staying at to the ground. That's why Alira's here."

I glance over at Alira. She has a smile on her face that seems more like a grimace.

Amber drops her hands to her lap, and finishes, "We met up with Desoto shortly after, and he trained me."

Amber had quite the adventure to get to me, and now that I am myself again, I appreciate her story even more. She risked everything to reach me, and for that, I owe her.

"One tactic Desoto taught me was we cannot just waltz through these tunnels to the antechamber like we own the place. We need stealth. Keep to the shadows and attack from the shadows as the Tree Leapers do. Didn't you learn that?"

I remember learning how to use my terrain to my advantage, but this is a new concept, so I let Amber teach it to me. She delves into some of the teachings Desoto also taught her. She tells me nine traits that this Light Spirit gives, also explaining that they helped her to restrain herself when I lashed out and ordered her to fight me. How I wish I could take back all that I said!

"No worries, Mike. I forgive you."

I notice the change in her, and I want to have this same peace. "You're different Amber, but you're still you. There is this light in your eyes that may have been there before, but now it's shining like a sun." In the minimal light, I see her wipe her eyes. "Hey, what's the matter?"

"Nothing. I'm just happy to see you analyzing again." She hugs me. "I'm so glad to have you back!"

I return the hug, but I cannot help wondering, did she have some doubts before? I don't blame her if she did, but I am a little saddened that she was skeptical that I was myself a few minutes ago. Now she knows for certain, which makes us both joyous.

We talk, and she teaches me everything Desoto taught her. "You catch on a lot quicker than I did, Mike."

I feel a sense of pride swell up. Amber smiles, pulling on imaginary reigns, and I understand. *Keep humble.* I tell myself.

The hour when we break free of this hellhole arrives with Amber leading the way. The first few tunnels pose no danger, since no one really comes down this way. Who would? It's dank, depressing, and dim; still, we press on, creeping forward in cautious silence, our feet dancing in light steps across the stone floor to avoid the echo of plodding.

A light dances before us, so we hit the wall. The light grows. Amber motions for us to shuffle down the tunnel. The orange glow chases shadows towards us. Amber pulls up her hood, and I can guess why. If we're seen, we can pass as new recruits. Alira and I do the same, but I hold my breath as the orange glow draws closer. I look up into the face of Lepez. He opens his mouth to rat us out, but Amber acts before the words can form on his tongue. She kicks him in the stomach, and then wallops him on the back of his head with a gauntlet. Lepez drops to the floor, out cold, and I pick up the torch.

"C'mon, we don't have much time. When this man doesn't return, Bastille will suspect something's amiss," Amber says standing.

She breaks into a slow jog and light floods the tunnel. I know where we are, so I step in front of my sister. If my mental layout is correct, we're two steps from entering the antechamber. "Amb, the obstacle course may not be the quickest, or the easy way out, but it is safer."

Amber shakes her head. "If we weren't pressed for time, Mike, I'd take you up on that. But since we are, I suggest we use the main entrance."

We make a dash for the entrance, when a Tree Leaper gives us away, but we do not stop.

Amber dives into the hole and I follow after Alira. Behind us, we hear hastened footfalls. A hand grasps my ankle. I kick with the other foot, and the hand releases me.

We burst into the twilight of the Shadow Flames. We're standing there in full alert, and Alira suddenly gasps. She's facing the wall where we came out, and she's backing away from it towards the flames. Her horror is written all over her expression.

Alarmed, I turn to face the tunnel, but no one is crawling through. I look up, down, around, mystified. She grabs my shoulder and points to the sloping wall beside the entrance to the tunnel. I raise the torch illuminating a cave painting. Haltingly, I attempt to translate the pictures. "Hunters fighting a really ugly centipede. So what's so alarming about that?"

"City fellas," Alira groans at my obtuseness. "It says *Flee* the Centipede."

"How do you see that?"

"The hunters are not fighting it, they are *running* from it. See, it is eating them."

I examine the picture closer. Alira's translation makes better sense than mine.

"All right, we've seen the warning, now let's go!" Amber hisses.

Alira and I nod. Amber turns to run. She reaches for Alira, and we form a chain. Then Amber charges through the Shadow Flames. Sunlight blinds me, but I do not let go of Alira's hand. Not until Amber slows to a walk. She circles the flames and heads for a grove of Eucalyptus trees. There we catch our breath. I watch her grab her bag from a hollow in a nearby tree. Then she slides to the ground chuckling. Her laughter intoxicates Alira and me, and soon the three of us are throwing our joys to the heavens. We escaped Bastille's domain, and we're alive to tell about it!

As we calm, wiping our eyes, I know the joy we feel now is temporary. We have to face Bastille again. Only the next time we do, she will be prepared for us. We will be walking into a war for this continent. I, no, we need a plan.

"It's risky, but this might work. When Desoto trained me, he said that Bastille could not see a person's motives. So Michael, you could say you've had a change of heart and walk in no problem."

"No, she will want proof, which will most likely be your head on a spear, and I'm not willing to do that."

"We must have switched roles, because I'm the one playing analyst now. Think, Mike, there must be many avenues to give her the proof she wants."

The wheels spin in my head. Steam screams from pressure values. Possibilities pour into the chute, but all that comes out the other end is slag. I think harder. The machine groans, and bulges. The pressure values burst, and then... nothing.

"Sorry Amb, I've got nothing." I say.

My sister doesn't let me throw in the towel, but draws my attention to her cloak by plucking at it. She plants the idea of Joseph and his twelve brothers in my head, and the light bulb blares, but then it dies again. I know what she wants me to do, because in the story, Joseph's brother's (who were jealous of him, because their father favored him over them) took the colorful cloak his father made for him and dipped it in lamb's blood. They presented the cloak to their father saying they found it in the fields. Amber wants me to do this with her cloak.

"But suppose Bastille knows that story? Suppose she realizes the blood isn't human, but say, a wallaby's? She'd know you're still alive. Then again, what if she doesn't? Instead of me selling you to a caravan of slave traders, you're sneaking through the obstacle course unannounced and unknown to her and the others in there."

"That's more the Michael I know. Analyzing every possible outcome. It'll work. Trust me."

"How do you know, Amb? What if she knows the story?"

"What if a Kiwi's sheep decided to overrun his farm and start practicing democracy?"

"How can sheep practice democracy?" Alira asks.

"They can't. Amber was making a point." I reply.

"Which is?"

"I said 'what if', which is just a way of playing an excuse card to not try to do something."

"I think I get it, and I do like her idea."

I do too, I just have this suspicion Bastille will know the story and that she will see through the act. Still, Amber is correct. The worst that can happen is she does know, and I have to smile and run. Then it occurs to me. Amber said she could see me in her mind. I wonder aloud if she could communicate with me as well.

Amber abruptly dismisses my contemplations, "Not sure, and we don't have time to try it right now. I'm gonna fetch us something for supper, and we'll dip my cloak in the carcass after. I'll even shred it to make it more believable. Can you and Ali make a fire?"

I nod and she disappears into the brush.

Amber returns with a joey, and I give her a look reminding her about our pact we made by the lake. She nods letting me know she has not forgotten about the agreement. I realize we need more blood than we'd get from a fairywren for our ruse to work, so I don't argue. Besides, there's meat around, and it's more than a fairywren. I prepare the joey. We work smoothly together, and inside of thirty minutes we sit down to eat.

My thought drift to the pictograph we saw on the wall in Ayers Rock. "What do you think that drawing means? And who drew it?"

"Michael, we know what it means. It's a warning that tells people to stay away. As for who drew it that's a little ambiguous, don't you think?" Alira wipes some juice from her hands.

Alira has a point, but that would imply that whoever drew the pictograph knew about Bastille. The only person we know who did know is Uli.

"You reckon Uli drew those paintings?"

"It's possible." Amber said covering her mouth with her hand. "But remember he ran from an opal stone in a cavern."

"I saw two halves of an opal stone at the bottom of the Spring of Rebirth, and under it was the remains of a hand. There was also a pickaxe, not far from it. Maybe that is how Bastille got loose. The person came across the stone, attempted to mine it, and Bastille did the rest. The stone must have fallen into that pool and split in two. Come to think about it, I saw a hole in the wall the size of that stone."

"It makes sense, but how does it tie into the drawings?"

"That's easy," Alira says. "Our ancestors came across the Centipede and ran out in fear. They told their tribe and those who believed drew the warning on the wall."

"Not to be a kill joy, but why does this apply to us? We are going back in there anyway, aren't we? So why are we even discussing this?" Amber interjects.

"Perhaps there is a clue in the drawings about how to defeat Bastille. Why else would Tree Leapers call it the Centipede's Nest?"

Amber shrugs, and suggests we rest up then head out. Alira seconds the motion. On the other hand, I request a little more time to perfect the technique of attacking from the shadows. Amber approves, saying we can all use some more training.

CHAPTER 11 Time's Up Tykes

AMBER

THREE PEOPLE CRAMMED INTO ONE TENT beats sleeping on the floor of a cave. Michael and Alira still asleep, murmur beside me. Well, I suppose I can fetch brekkie. I decide, it's better than staring at the ceiling.

My limbs still ache from the preparations we accomplished last night, but if I know Michael, he's going to wonder where lunch is when he wakes, so I sit up and throw on some pants. Trying to keep the noise I make to a minimum, my ruckus rouses Alira, and I apologize for waking her.

"Don't worry about it." She whispers, probably because she doesn't want to wake up Michael. I tell her she can use her normal voice because he'll sleep through a foghorn, and she giggles. "By the way, where're you going?"

"To fetch something for brekkie to go with that left over joey. Wanna come with?"

"No thank-you, I'll stay here."

"Suit yourself," I say vacating the tent. "If Michael wakes, tell him I'm grabbing him some more grub."

Alira nods, and I scout out across the Outback.

The sun peeks over Ayers Rock bathing the plain in a yellow-orange glow, but the red sands in the gloom below remind of a mat of chocolate. In the distance, the drum roll of the Shadow Flames rumbles in a gentle breeze. For a moment, there is tranquility, no thylacine or Tree Leapers around to dampen the feeling. I can search for breakfast in peace.

I take a deep breath of crisp morning air, and then I spot it in the morning glow. Keeping my steps light, I creep closer to the sleeping animal, and extend the Geckos ready for anything, attack or flight. My foot snaps a twig, but the animal does not stir. That's weird. It should have darted up. I walk closer. In the increasing light, I see a hand. A human hand.

I make a ruckus to rouse whomever it is laying on the ground, but he doesn't budge. I gently jolt the person with my foot, and he flops over onto his stomach. A dagger is protruding from his back.

I turn my back on the body and flee the crime scene struggling to contain a scream.

I burst into our camp where I let the scream I'd held in out in a long, high pitched wail. Michael pokes his head out the tent flap glowering and grumping at me. He is not appreciating the rude awakening, but at this point I don't care. I saw a man laying dead on the plain. Pegged by a dagger. Michael's beauty sleep can wait!

Every detail is etched in stark facets in my brain. The horror chokes words in my throat, and while I want to tell them everything, nothing but gasps and whimpers pour from my mouth. I flap my hands and press them against my lips pacing the camp.

For the moment, Michael's ire is quenched and he encourages, "Amb, take a deep breath."

I do, and it helps. Soon I find my voice. It's shaky, but I find it. "I saw... a man. Lying... on the ground... dead."

"How do you know he was dead?" Alira smiles at Michael, "How do you know he wasn't just a heavy sleeper like Michael?" Her pearly whites exposed, and her expression the picture of innocence. He does the same, though his radiates with sarcasm.

"I saw a dagger protruding from his back." I reply, my voice quivering.

Alira blanches in disgust, but my news intrigues my twin. He wants to see the body to identify it. Since I'm not going back there, I point in the direction I came from wishing him luck in his expedition.

"You're not coming?"

"Nope. I'd rather stay here and stare at a fire than look at that inhumane sight again. The killer did not even bother to bury the body."

Michael brings a chilling theory to the table. "What if the killer did not bury the body, because he *wanted* you or me to find it?"

Naturally, my mind starts churning out questions. Questions that I wonder if I actually want to know the answers to, or do I want to remain ignorant. Whether the killer meant for me to find the body or not, I have a suspect and a victim in mind. A hunch, I pray will be wrong.

"Amb, you know where the body is. The least you can do is show me where you saw it."

"Nope. Sorry Mike, you're on your own for this one."

"And if I get captured by Tree Leapers again?"

Ooh, he would pull that line! He's right too, because I want him at my side. I want him safe from those creeps, and how can I keep him safe if I'm not with him? War breaks out within me. I want to stay by his side in case any Tree Leaper or murderer decides to show back up. But to see the body again in all the gruesomeness, would I be able to stomach the sight? Now, it takes a lot to make me chunder. Even with Vegemite, though appalling in every way, I can still keep my lunch down. However, when I saw that body, I could taste the searing acid rising in my throat.

I stifle a sigh. "All right, you win, but only because I want to keep peace and not lose you again," I say. A smile crosses his face.

The person lay in the same position I left him with the dagger still jutting up from between the back of his ribs.

Michael researched human anatomy, and he says, "That dagger pierced his heart. He was probably dead before he hit the ground."

I keep my back to him while Alira investigates the person with my brother. Then

Alira gasps, and instinctively I turn around. Michael has rolled the body over onto its side. It's Desoto. Huge tears blur my vision, and I swipe at them. I don't understand. I prayed against this! Why would Yesh, let him die?

I called him to be with me. He completed what I called him to do. When it was time, he asked me to take his spirit.

But I needed him!

No Amber, the person you needed was your brother. Desoto taught you what he knew. For my glory, he obeyed me. Now it is time to teach your brother the same tactics, so the two of you can complete the task Uli gave you.

The torch passes from one teacher to the next. From Desoto to me, but I still wish he was here with me, so that if I misdirected my brother he could correct me. Yesh tells me not to worry, but trust in him and that he will give me the words to say to my brother. You would think by now that I have grasped this aspect of trusting Yesh, but it's not as easy as you think. Most of the time I'm a fish following a dancing light in the deep sea (only this light, the Light Spirit, isn't going to lead me to the jaws of the enemy).

We mourn the loss of Desoto. I take one final look at his serene face as Michael builds a fire around his body to cremate him. I stare at the smoke column billowing toward the heavens. I suppose it is the humane thing to do rather than have his body decompose or be torn to pieces by dingoes, but he was like a second father to me, and I will miss his teachings, his knowledge of Yesh. Michael squeezes my shoulder sympathetically, and I lean on him wringing my eyes of every tear. Before I met Yesh, you would not catch me shedding a single tear at a funeral. Guess he's softening my heart as he works in my life.

"Well, well, well. Look what the dingoes dragged out of the hole. Another traitor. And here I thought you had such potential, mate."

The three of us spin around. Zietas. He would show up and crash the funeral as we're saying good-bye to my teacher. His hood covers his face. It must be embarrassing to walk around with one eye!

Zietas runs a talon along the edge of his scimitar. "Hello, tykes?" I just glare at him. "Oh come now, is this any way to treat your Uncle Zietas."

"Save it Cyclops! We know you killed Desoto." Michael snaps, and I snicker.

Zietas sheaths his scimitar and presses his fingers against his talons placing them under his nose. I want those metal claws to lodge themselves in his nose, so I can slay him while he's occupied with removing them.

"I was hoping to find your girlfriend, so I could bring her to you, but it looks like she found you on her own. Tell me, Amber, how was it when you walked through the Shadow Flames? Did you feel like turning around? Running for your life and forgetting everything?"

The question seems rhetorical, so why waste my breath answering it? His way of popping up at the most inconvenient moments is starting to irk me.

He waggles his talons, "I reckon you did, and I reckon your legs felt like they were attached to an iron ball as you stumbled aimlessly in the darkness.

"In fact, I know you felt that temptation, because Desoto felt the same thing when he left. He told me during our little reunion."

Funny how you can recognize lies for what they are when you have, Yesh.

Zietas stroked his chin, "What were the words he told me before I ran him through? Oh, yes: 'You may have won this skirmish Zietas, but you've lost the war!' Ha! How wrong he was! The war has been won since the day the Centipede created the Shadow Flames."

I glower at Zietas pointing my gauntlets at his chest, while Alira draws her bow. Michael aims for Zietas' face.

Michael asks, "Just what exactly are the Shadow Flames?"

Come to think of I don't know either. We've seen thylacine spawned from them. A perentie walked in and came out a Komodo dragon, and ghosts of ourselves with sickles for hands (I've seen the last one, but you know what I mean).

Zietas folds his arms and looks at the ground snickering. He stops abruptly, reaching for his scimitar, "Are you that stupid, Amber? Remember when we fought him in Simpsons Gap? No matter how hard you tried, you could not lay a scratch on me."

That was just yesterday actually. Ignoring his comment, I repeat my brother's question.

"I suppose I can part with that information, seeing as you won't be able to use the knowledge because you'll be lying in a pool of each other's blood. The Shadow Flames are a living fire. They were created by the Centipede to birth the life of the past. It will transform Australia into what it was before man came and tainted it with colonization. When the fires are loosed, everything from the Komodo to the lesser bilby will roam these lands once more, and man will come close to extinction on this continent! Only those committed to serving the Centipede will survive."

"So what of the doppelgangers my sister faced? How are they linked to the past?" Michael asks.

"They are simply another means to exterminate the human race, nothing more."

Though that information is useful I am more concerned with his answer to the first question. Mainly, that Centipede. I reckon Zietas means that drawing of the giant centipede we saw on Ayers Rock. Still, while Zietas' ear-bashes, I look to Yesh for guidance and strength. How can I defeat Zietas?

I will fight for you. You need only be still.

Be still? Zietas will slay me if I be still!

By your own strength you can do nothing, but through me all things are possible.

Yet, this isn't impossible. I can defeat Zietas. Bastille maybe a different story, but Zietas is an arrogant pig, whose reward was spelled out when he joined that demon queen. His self-proclaimed invincibility to us will be his downfall, right?

Amber, I warn you to not underestimate this man. What you saw in Simpsons Gap was only a fraction of his capabilities.

If that was a fraction of what he could do, then do I want to know his full capabilities?

He draws strength from the Darkness. Trust in me and do not lean on your own judgment. Allow me to guide your hands and your feet so that you may evade his blade.

I open my eyes and look into Zietas' shadowed face.

"Have you finished conversing with Desoto's imaginary comrade, Amber? Are you ready to meet his fate?"

"No, Zietas, today, if Yesh shall have it, your blood will be spilled."

The words shock Michael and Alira and me. Since when do I talk like that? Regardless, I feel stronger, full of a new life, so I reckon Yesh must be working through me. I raise my Geckos again. Zietas utters a hollow laugh swaying with his head facing the ground, one hand on his scimitar. These actions seem to be a mockery, as he keeps his cake hole shut, but the incessant laughter wears on me. Definitely jeering, but I hold my ground.

Zietas finally speaks, his head rolling to expose his left eye. The eye appears to glow red in the shadows of his hood. "Bold words for a novice. We will see who lives to speak of this day."

Hands gripping his scimitar, he rushes me.

CHAPTER 12 Treachery And Tyranny

MICHAEL

ZIETAS CHARGES AMBER, HIS FEET LIGHT and swift. I fire a round at him to draw his attention, but his sights remain on my sister. Alira looses an arrow. Zietas deflects it without turning his head. He slashes at my sister keeping her on the defensive. His skill deadly and unmatched by anything earthly I've ever seen. His precision is consistent and continuous. I search for openings in his defense, so I run around to his back while Amber occupies him from the front. I need to be quick or Zietas will run her through, yet his steps are so erratic that I cannot get a clear shot, so I fire blind praying I hit him. The blade grazes him and sails into the dirt at his feet. Zietas stops, and turns to me. Amber takes the breath she needed, while this supernatural warrior walks toward me. Though blood trickles from his wound, he seems oblivious to it. I ready myself.

An arrow sails for Zietas from behind me. Slicing, his sword a blur, he sends the arrow to the ground in two pieces, which drop like dead weight. The gap between us closes, as I frantically reload my blades. Alira steps to my side, while Amber charges him recklessly. Zietas turns and extends his sword, but Amber does something not even I saw coming. She slides. Her head passes within an inch of the tip of his sword. As she slides past, she slashes his legs. Zietas stumbles, and I see my chance. I loose a blade, and it slips under his guard imbedding in Zietas' side. We found the holes in his seemingly flawless defense!

Staggering, Zietas yanks my blade from his ribs, his lips curling into a sardonic smile. His silent rage poisons that smile, and with the strength of a lion he hurls the blade back at me. Thankfully, he misses, but his throw drives the blade deep into the trunk of a Eucalyptus. I stare for a second at the blade contemplating the injury I would have sustained had he hit me! Turning back to Zietas, I see him heaving and holding his ribs.

"It's over Zietas, you've lost!" Amber says.

Zietas just laughs again. Alira fires an arrow, probably to clam him up, but as before, he sends it for the dirt. Then he drops to his knees turning his face to the sky. I see the monstrosity his face has become. He screams in a tongue I've never heard before. He takes his daggers from their sheaths and slashes his wrists simultaneously, and then falls face down in the dirt. A demonic ritual no doubt, and I can guess to whom. He's probably praying to Bastille to take his soul.

Then he stands up wounds dripping and makes for the Shadow Flames. He doesn't flee; he just walks toward them. Alira raises her bow. She looses an arrow at his back, but as Zietas stumbles, he continues to walk for the Flames. He reaches for the arrow and removes it, but does not turn around. Amber gets to her feet, brushing her hair behind her ear, as she follows Zietas, so I run up to her.

"What are you doing?" I demand grabbing her wrist and turning her around.

"Mike, this may sound crazy, but if we don't stop Zietas, he will kill Bastille."

"That's great! It means we don't have to do it." Then I see the urgency and confusion in her eyes as she shakes her head. "You mean that ritual he just did was a, "

"According to Yesh, that was directed to his king. Zietas plans to overthrow Bastille, and take whatever power she possesses for himself. When Zietas spoke in that tongue, Yesh translated for me. 'Take my soul into your bosom, my King. Grant me the power you gave to your passive servant, so that I may slay her and complete the work you set out for her! Leave her and come into me!'

"Mike, if we don't stop him all will be lost. Should Zietas succeed in slaying Bastille he'll release the Shadow Flames. They will scatter like a nuclear bomb consuming all of Australia!"

My eyes widen in terror. I may not know this Light Spirit yet, but Amber seems to know him, and believes everything he says. So far, he has guided her and led her directly to me. I did have the same dream she did, and I did see that giant thylacine's skull rise from the Shadow Flames as they spread out like a shock wave. If what she claims is true, I don't want to sit around and wait for the world to end. I nod, and after we explain the situation to Alira, the three of us chase after Zietas.

A hissing growl stops us in our tracks. I guard the girls, but Amber insists on standing at my side. I instruct everyone to stand back to back, and move in formation. I point my gauntlets guarding their backs as I assume they are guarding mine. The growling continues from a hollow of rocks before me, so I ball a fist. The theory is to scare whatever is behind the small crag. My knife ricochets off the rock with a soft ping, and a loud, territorial hiss follows.

"Any ideas what it is?" Amber whispers in my ear.

"I have an idea."

"Okay...?"

"I'll give you a hint, it's a lizard and rhymes with tomato."

"Does it see us?"

"Probably n... probably. Definitely. Hey Ali, how good is your aim?" A large head twice the size of a Komodo dragon emerges from behind the rock. The head stands about knee-height. I swallow nervously.

Amber locks her gaze upon it, too. Alira steps back and turns to run. Sharply, I call out her name. She stops, poised to run.

"Alira, if you run, it's like urging it to give chase. This thing can only be one thing, the king of goannas: the megalania. Be very careful. I read that recent research shows they were venomous."

"I see it, and I'm not liking it." Amber says.

"How do we get by it without it chasing us." Alira asks.

"Slowly, and keep your eye on it."

"But once we pass the rock how will we know if it is hunting us?"

"We'll see it. Now slowly, let's go"

Alira nods, and Amber bumps me elbow to elbow. I motion the girls to begin walking, while I hold back briefly to keep an eye on the giant goanna. Then I, too, slowly follow the girls. My pace quickens as the distance between me and the Megalania lengthens, so far, he does not appear to be following me, but then again goannas, or sometimes called monitor lizards, tend to do just that: laze around watching you until you least expect it, then they ambush you.

I read that Komodos have bacteria in their saliva that attacks their victim's immune system over the course of a few hours, since it spreads so quickly the body cannot keep up and the victim eventually dies. Then the Komodo having stood by watching for sometimes days calls his mates and they feast! I'm willing to bet my life the Megalania (extinct, I might add) has similar predatory tactics, so I do not want to take my eye off him for too long, or it's lights out for me. Possibly, lights out for the girls as well considering we're not as large as say, a water buffalo.

I glance over my shoulder to see the Megalania emerging from the rocks. "Amb, Ali you may wanna turn around."

My sister stops and slowly turns around. She points her blades at the beast, and Alira notches an arrow. I take aim, letting out a controlled breath as I ball a fist. The workings of my gauntlets groan slightly then the blade springs free from its casing. It flies for the lizard's head impaling it. With a roar, the lizard rushes us.

"Ace, Mike! You ticked him off!" Amber says.

"Just shoot him!" I retort.

She does, aiming for his eyes. She misses, and tries again. No eyes means no sight, and a quicker victory for us. Meanwhile Alira fires arrows at his legs. The lizard lunges for me. I narrowly manage to evade the scythe-like nails by leaping over them and mounting the beast. I drive my knives into his sides repeatedly. As blood pours from the wounds, he staggers.

Alira shoots one final round into his eye, and he collapses. Amber makes the finishing blow by driving her blades into his heart. Blood and water spurt from the wound. The Megalania is dead.

"Next time, don't shoot at it," breathes my sister.

"I had no choice. I'll give you an example. A perentie can run up to thirty kilometers an hour while inflating its lungs with balloon-like muscles in its neck, so if we started to flee, think of the top speed of this monster."

"All right, so maybe your option was the better one, but next time warn me will ya?"

I nod. "Now let's get back to chasing down Zietas before he slays Bastille."

Bodies litter Bastille's domain. We're too late. Zietas has already been here. He's already obtained Bastille's power.

I cast a glance at my sister, her eyes dart about surveying the tragedies.

One man, still holding on, calls out, "Michael, over here." Despite his state, I recognize Lepez. I lean in close. He can barely speak, "Michael, be... beware the... cen... beware the Centipede..." His hands curl, and his eyes widen in fear. I looked behind me, nothing there. When I look back at Lepez, his face is frozen in agony from something I can't see.

I stay with Lepez for a little while placing his hands on his chest. Guilt creeps down my spine. I don't know why I feel so guilty. It just washes through me leaving anxiety. I don't understand why his expression is so horror struck. Amber places a hand on my shoulder, we lock eyes, and I nod standing.

"What is the meaning of this, Zietas?" We hear Bastille's voice echo through the shaft from her chamber.

Amber and I exchange looks then scramble for Bastille's chambers. Alira wants to come too, but Amber orders her to stay put, this is something we must do alone. Though her aid would be useful, I reckon she might end up seeing someone in the pool like I did and jump in, so I agree with Amber. Her best option is to stay in the antechamber and fend off anyone who might walk in. We'll scrabble through the obstacle course while the voices of Bastille and Zietas echo through the tunnels.

"You're slow Bastille. In the time it has taken you to gather an army, those two you sent me out to slay have," I assume he's referring to us, "grown stronger. They are in hot pursuit to put an end to this. You've become soft. I'm finishing what you should have done centuries ago!"

"Is that any way to address your queen? Don't turn this blame on me Zietas. I gave you the order to slay them and you did not."

"You are no longer my queen, Bastille! He's shouting, "Perhaps not killing them was my fault. That still doesn't excuse your faults of allowing them to discover your flames. You had the chance to cleanse this continent when the first settlers landed, but you chose to laze around Uluru."

"You heard Michael in the tunnel. He could see the flames because he had that bumbling buffoon's blood flowing through his veins. They would have seen it and acted upon it anyway. Now, bow before me or I will slay you where you stand!"

Zietas shouts to Bastille in that strange tongue again.

My sister says, "Let's use the quickest way to her chamber."

I point to the hole in the ceiling. I scramble up the wall with Amber close behind me. I leap through the hole to see Zietas rushing Bastille in combat. Both use swords. Talk about déjà vu! Then Zietas pins his former queen and raises his hand. His fingers lengthen and become one long shaft. Turning mustard-yellow, it files into a point, while Bastille stares in horror. Then, with the Centipede leg formed, he falls on her, driving the leg into her heart. He twists it sealing her death.

"We're too late!" Amber says as she sinks to her knees.

Zietas looks up, and then turns to face us. An evil grin creases his lips. We are too late. He stands extending his arms, and shouts another chant in that tongue. I ask Amber to translate, but she shakes her head, probably too frightening, I reckon.

The Shadow Flames envelope Zietas, he laughs maliciously receiving the power. The laughter deepens mingling with a snarl.

I load my gauntlets. Amber stands and braces herself. Though she tries to contain it, I can see her knees shaking. We're terrified, and who wouldn't be? Our adversary is transforming before us into the demon he always aspired to be.

CHAPTER 13 The Centipede's Wrath

MICHAEL

NIGHTMARES BECOME REALITY. A giant ram-horned skull of a thylacine with green eyes juts out from the flames. The eyes cast an eerie glow about the room. He roars. Then we see Zietas' torso, emaciated and death-grey, rises awkwardly towards the roof of the chamber. His metal talons compliment a cadaverous hand with black nails. He raises both hands glorifying himself. His torso morphs into the tar-coloured body of the Centipede with pairs of mustard-yellow legs the size of my forearm. It scuttles from the flames!

The menace of our nightmare finally rears his ugly head! Zietas towers above us, his face is that petrified skull from our dream. It has that ghastly jagged grin. He contorts his body, and opens his jaw to let out the infamous cry of the thylacine as a growl resonates up from the belly of Hell.

We take aim, and fire at Zietas, reload, and fire again, but he bats away the projectiles as if they are mere twigs. Amber tries a different tactic while I continue to fire blade after blade at Zietas. She rushes him, and though he tries to multi-task, we have the upper hand. Amber amputates as many centipede legs that she can reach. Her Gecko blades flashing so fast they blur. I finally puncture his defensive tactics, and my knives slice through his segments. Then just when we think we have him backed up against the cliff, Zietas plays dirty.

He bats Amber aside with his tail sending her tumbling for the shaft. I run to grab her, but Zietas tackles me to the ground before I reach my sister, and she slides down the tunnel. Metal scrapes along the tunnel, so I assume she is attempting to slow her descent.

Zietas lifts me into the air and throws me against the rock face. The blow winds me, and like a rag doll, I crumple to the ground groaning and folded over in pain. Zietas laughs at my efforts to regain footing while he wallops me again, but this time I manage to slash at his hand, and flee to the other end of the room.

Metal shrieks across the stone, and I glance over my shoulder, as Amber emerges from the hole. She draws Zietas into the Rebirthing Spring chamber, probably to let me regain my ground. I struggle to follow her, but with blows still throbbing all over my body, my steps falter.

Stumbling through the tunnel, I can hear her conflict with Zietas. Hang in there Amb, I'll be at your side soon. A splash. Zietas must have knocked her into the spring, but my legs are as iron chains, each step is like dragging a hundredweight straight up a cliff face. I must keep pressing forward no matter the pain. The last step I take into the chamber consumes most of my strength, so I lean in the archway recovering. I watch Amber battle Zietas. Water is dripping from her clothes. I draw in a breath, which is like a crushing weight to my lungs, then I raise my gauntlets to Zietas' skull.

"How ya goin', you great oaf! Did you forget about me?" I holler.

Zietas stops and turns opening his jaw, as coherent words bellow from some supernatural force within him. "I did not forget about you Michael, I simply left you to die in that chamber, but now I see I should have finished you off!" His voice is different. The timbre is silky and deeper, demonic. I wonder if it is Zietas talking or the Centipede. I decide it is probably a combination of the two, but I don't know for certain.

Zietas charges me, one hundred-some-odd legs tapping the rock floor sounding like rain on a sidewalk. For a few seconds, Amber gets the breather she needs. Then she presses on to aid me.

Zietas rears up, his face towering out of reach, so I go for his legs. He dives for me and I slash at his skull. Green light floods my face, as Zietas roars holding the gash in his skull. The wound tells me we can win this fight! I smile. Amber settles by my side, and we ready ourselves.

Zietas falls to the ground. A wall of Shadow Flames rolling in the corner of the room billows up somewhat and the Centipede scuttles into them disappearing from our sight.

"Coward! Come back and fight us!" I call. Then I realize Amber isn't at my side. "Amb, where'd you, "

"C'mon Mike we don't have to dilly dally."

"You know where Zietas went?"

"Does the nightmare mean anything to you?"

My eyes widen as I recollect the thylacine skull screaming above the Shadow Flames as they churn like a tsunami for civilization. "Well, what're we standing here for? How do we go after him?"

"Same way we got in."

"No bull, right?"

"Right. Now come on."

"What about Ali?"

"Her, too. Now, come on!"

We meet up with Alira in the antechamber; she is relieved to see us, and she asks if we defeated Bastille and Zietas.

"Long-story short, Bastille's dead and Zietas is that giant centipede we saw on the cave wall. He is even now scuttling to wipe out civilization as we know it. We don't have much time. Let's go."

Alira surprisingly accepts everything we tell her without question, and follows us out of the tunnel. A low rumble precedes a deafening crack. Dust falls on our heads. I look up into a large crack creeping across the ceiling.

That can't be good.

My prediction proves true when the crack widens and races towards our only exit. It divides into several smaller branches like the mouth of a river. The tunnel rumbles. Rocks scrape against each other threatening a cave-in. I open my mouth to order the girls to run for the exit, but they're already scrambling for the exit. The Shadow Flames burst into the tunnel washing over us.

Linking hands, we press forward stumbling over each other until we break free landing in a heap on the red sands surrounding The Rock. We get to our feet and brush ourselves off when what sounds like an incessant belch from Shadow Flames bursts across the plains. They curl furiously into the heavens.

Tree Leapers run from the collapsing caverns meeting us outside stumbling into us and around us. Some cast dirty looks at us while others run in terror across the plain. Amid the panic, I do not see Hol. Filled with a heroic intuition, I charge back into the tunnel. Behind me, I hear Amber screaming for me to come back, but if Hol is trapped beneath a rock, I want to save her life even if she was crude to me.

Inside the collapsing caverns, I holler for her. I scurry through the tunnel before me. "Hol! Where are you?"

"Who's there, and how do you know my name?"

"It's Michael. Where are you?"

"Shove off, traitor! I don't need your help!" I follow the sound of her voice to the ropes course. Then I see her tangled in the ropes like a fly in a web amid rocks crashing into the pool. Her sneer softens. "Get outta here you dill. You don't want to save me." But I advance toward her loading my gauntlets. "You gonna kill me like a coward? You'll never have a better chance, you know." She squirms in the ropes.

A large chunk of rock splits in two at my feet. Only one of the pieces disappears with a splash into the water. I breathe, cutting her loose.

"Why'd you risk your life to save me? You know I could kill you right now and dump you into the pool."

"But you won't. You are probably grateful *someone* came back for you."

"You're smarter than ya look kid. Now let's get outta here before we both become trapped."

She doesn't have to convince me. I run ahead of her. Then a piece of the tunnel separates her from me. "Go on! Get outta here!"

"I'm not leaving you." I reply trying to move the boulder as the tunnel continues to cave in.

"Leave, I'm tellin' ya. I deserve to die in here. If you really knew me, you would agree."

"C'mon, Hol, don't say that."

"I *am* saying it, because before I came here I was a crime boss. I lied, I cheated people of their dough, and I even committed murder on several occasions. Trust me, I'm a no good person. It's better this way."

"Even the people who commit the greatest crimes can be redeemed." I say. Then I realize what I said. Since when did I use words like redeemed. Come to think of it, what drove me to save this woman in the first place?

I did. I planted the idea in your head and you acted upon it.

It doesn't take much brainpower to realize that Amber's friend, Yesh, had just spoken to me, and though I'm amazed he would, I still don't understand why.

You've done what you can Michael. Now leave this cavern before it caves on you.

"But what about Hol?"

"What about me, what?" I hear her from the other side of the stone. I suddenly realize I said that aloud.

"Never mind." I say. Then talk in my head to this Light Spirit. What about Hol?

I will reason with her; if she desires, she will listen, but you must leave now.

I take off down the tunnel, expecting to hear Hol scream after me to help her move the rock, but she never calls out. I reckon Yesh must be talking with her. Maybe, whether she chooses to let him set her free, or seal her fate in this dank, dark network, I will never know her fate.

The antechamber collapses around me. I stop and try to search out an exit. The only two exits I know about are that shaft you crawl through and the one by the obstacle course. Both of those exits are blocked. My thoughts race and tumble.

How did Zietas reach Bastille in such a short time? He wasn't running. I try to visualize what I saw in that grove. He walked towards the Shadow Flames, and by the time we reached Ayers Rock, he'd already slain most of his comrades. How did he reach the rock that quickly? Could the Shadow Flames be a means of transportation as well?

I think back to our first encounter with Zietas. How did he find us? Amber said she recognized Desoto's voice when he was still following Bastille, so they must have used the Flames to inform Bastille then returned with a small posse to slay us. It was worth a shot. Besides, I was running out of options.

The ceiling around Bastille's tunnel collapses.

No way! Could it be that Yesh did that?

The ceiling ruptures above me, and I decide to just accept the miracle and make for the tunnel. Once in her chambers, I head for the Shadow Flames in the Rebirthing Spring chamber. The flames churn and roar before me. I breathe, and charge into the flames, and simply run into a wall. That doesn't work so I head back to the spring.

Evil Amber rises again from the pool. She beckons me to join her again, but this time I turn a blind eye and point my gauntlets at her face. The gesture angers her and she screams flying from the pool. I point my gauntlets toward her and close my eyes. Suddenly, she is silent. I open my eyes as she disintegrates before me.

The Rebirthing Spring churns and spirals into a whirlpool. The vortex consumes the pool, and I hear Yesh tell me to jump in. Amber trusts him, so I take the leap of faith. The vortex sucks me out of the chamber, and I see pieces of the giant opal swirling around me.

A minute later, though the time felt like hours, the vortex spits me out into a pool outside of Ayers Rock. The opal fragments, which are now a fine dust, glitter around me as they settle to the bottom of the pool. I swim for the shore, and a hand grabs me hauling me on dry land. Within seconds, Amber embraces me.

She says through tears, "Never, ever do that again!"

"I promise," I say heartily even though I don't believe I will ever have another experience such as that. It felt good to promise her anyway.

Deep booms and cracklings vibrate around me, and I notice the noise is coming from the flames. A loud crack rumbles across the plain then a large chunk of Ayers Rock dislodges and slides down, sealing the entrance to the catacombs.

Suddenly, the Shadow Flames spiral skyward forming the thylacine skull we saw in our dream.

Looking up at the skull, I say, "Amb, any ideas?"

"Working on it."

"Amb, if you've got anything, do it now!" The Centipede lifts his head to the sky.

"Right," she nods at me then cups her hands around her mouth amplifying her voice. "Oy! Ugly! Remember us? Come finish what you started! Unless the King of the Shadow Flames would rather show all his followers the coward he really is?"

Though I half expected Yesh to flood my sister and levitate her up to Zietas, that doesn't happen. Zietas does turn in our direction. Amber puffs out her chest and throws open her arms, as she steps forward challenging Zietas. He screams that thylacine yowl and charges down Ayers Rock, the centipede legs clacking against the rock. Tree Leapers rush us, so we fought them off slashing at their legs maiming them.

Boomerangs arc. Daggers fly with deadly accuracy directly toward our heads and bodies. Yet, somehow Amber and I manage to deflect them and evade it all.

Zietas bands with his forces and they enclose us in a ring. Three against a dozen and one giant centipede. Dismal odds. Behind us the Shadow Flames swell trying to break free of an invisible restraint, awaiting their king's consent to engulf civilization. We need a miracle to pull this off. Then Amber says something under her breath removing the chains from her thumbs.

"You say something?" I ask.

"Through me, you can do the impossible." She says slightly louder.

"What?"

"Through me you, "

"Yeah, I got that, but what?"

"Ye of little faith…" Amber says. Then she pushes through the ring, slashing two men with her blades, and makes for the bushes and sporadic acacia trees. Zietas chases her down. This looks familiar. "Mike, Ali, cover me." She tosses me her pouch of blades.

I catch them wondering what she has up her sleeve, but before I can discuss her plan with her, she is rushing Zietas with her arms extended and her blades pointed toward him. Yet she doesn't fire them, and I see the reason she tossed me her pouch. She doesn't need it. She only needs the two she has loaded in her gauntlets.

I empty her blades into my satchel. Then Alira and I open fire on Zietas while Amber engages him. I can tell he is struggling to counter everything. It doesn't take long for the Tree Leapers to surge against us. Alira and I are forced to turn our attention to the remaining Tree Leapers who fight for their king.

I feel horrible leaving Amber to take on Zietas alone, but if I help her, the Tree Leapers will take us out. We need a miracle to win this battle, a boost of strength, a pair of wings, anything. Suddenly the Tree Leapers stop, shake their heads, and drop their weapons. They look to Zietas then flee for the trees.

The King of Shadows sees this, and gives chase. The Shadow Flames dwindle and Zietas stumbles, so he turns ignoring the Tree Leapers, and returns to the flames.

The cogs in my brain try to comprehend what just happened. Then I remember the vortex obliterating the opal stone in the Spring of Rebirth. Amber hinted that the opal was used to indoctrinate people when she reiterated Desoto's testimony. Now, with that great opal stone destroyed, the Centipede no longer has power over the men and women hiding in the glade.

I glance back at the Shadow Flames that sputter and churn, yearning for their master's consent to vent. But Amber, Alira and I will not let Zietas pass. Strange to call him that because there is nothing of the man left in this great centipede hulk with a thylacine skull. The demon and fully taken over and transformed the man.

The Centipede rushes Alira and me, but we impale him with blades and arrows. While I load the blades, I glance at my sister. She clambers up onto his back using her blades to scale each segment up his torso. Zietas grunts and tries to knock her off. Each writhing movement opens up another segment for us to fire into, so he cannot do swipe off Amber *and* fend us off as well. His scream of frustration and pain splits the plain as he twists and reaches for my sister. She flails for a split second on his back then her gauntlets dig in deep.

She hollers, "Michael, kick Zietas in the segment closest to you!" Zietas flails and grabs in an attempt to dislodge my sister from his back.

I reckon a standard kick will hurt me more than it will him, so I charge to perform a standard round-house kick. Instead of nailing him with the side of my foot, I snap my foot in an arc nailing Zietas in the closest segment with the tip of my foot, a hook kick. The most forceful technique we know.

Zietas screams and falters snapping at me. As the huge head comes within range, I kick the side of his face with a side thrust kick. His jaw splinters. Zietas rears up, and Amber scales his torso.

She raises one blade, it glows pink in the afternoon sun, blood dripping from metal. She shouts, "Go back to the depths of the grave!" and drives the blade into his heart.

Zietas' hands open, his eyes brightly glimmer then dim an instant later. Time seems to slow as he staggers. He yowls again.

Anticipating the angle of his collapse, I order Alira to move out of the way. Frozen in fear, she just stands there. The centipede is writhing and falling. I can only pray I am not too late. I dive at her and we tumble out of the way. Zietas topples billowing dust into the air. When all settles, I roll off Alira, and carefully I lift her to her feet apologizing.

"What for? I am grateful you pushed me. He would have squashed me like a roach if you didn't act when you did." A grin brightens her face. Then she kisses my cheek, and shyly sways with her hands behind her back.

I smile, probably blushing, too, but I would rather attribute pink cheeks to the sunset reflection. My hand touches the spot where her lips touched my cheek.

Amber clears her throat. She removes her blade while standing atop our deceased foe then slides down his torso. I catch her. She wallops my shoulder. "Good on-ya Mike. Good on-ya!"

"I had a good teacher."

"No, that was you, mate. All you. I only told you to kick him. You chose the kicks to use and when and where to plant them."

My grin goes a little crooked, and I know my eyes are sparkling with satisfaction. It's a strong emotion that wells up in my chest that feels good like a job well done.

Then I take a gander at Zietas. His jaw litters the ground. His once glowing sockets are dark and vacant. His arms stretch across the ground, metal talons buried in the sand. His segments flatten a bramble. His legs are jutting out in a tangle, some twisted, others broken.

I walk over to his head. I had an idea based on the size of his body it was huge, but I am amazed it is my height and two of me in length! He could have easily swallowed me whole with that gape. I stare for several minutes.

Amber pats my back again. Alira embraces me. I beam. We won! We defeated Zietas! We vanquished the Centipede! I can just believe it, and if Amber did not have the guidance from Yesh, he probably *would* have squashed us like roaches.

Tree Leapers emerge from their hiding places cheering, but flee again because the earth suddenly shakes, and a guttural roar rattles the plain. The Shadow Flames roll inward as if to avoid an invisible deluge of water. The once great crowns now fall inwards, dwindling. Then a wind groans across the plain in gusts. Acacias bend toward the flames. The three of us begin to slide toward them.

"Run to the nearest tree and hang on!" I order.

We run. Shadow Flames swirl towards us. Tree Leapers latch onto the trees too, but the trees threaten to uproot.

I cast a glance at Amber and Alira. They've wrapped their legs around their tree. That idea is worth trying, so I do the same. Bushes up root and become tumbleweeds. Sand billows, stinging my eyes. Then the chaos ebbs.

Everything turns calm and Ayers Rock glows pink in the afternoon sun. Zietas' corpse is gone and the plain looks as it should look, barren and tranquil. Nothing remains of the fight for our lives. The Tree Leapers who survived the cave-in cheer.

Over the approval and applause, we hear a woman calling out to Alira. The three of us see Ira pushing through the crowd. Alira's face brightens, the crowd parts as the two hug.

"Amb this, "

"Is your mother," Amber says.

CHAPTER 14 Uli's Confession

AMBER

MICHAEL AND I SAY GOOD-BYE TO ALIRA and her mother, and I want to ask why she abandoned her daughter, but the two seem so happy with their reunion. Why spoil the moment?

"Why did you leave me, Mother?" Now I know how Michael must feel when I say out loud what he's thinking! I decide to eavesdrop; well, I guess I was already doing that.

"Please try to understand, my sweet Alira. I know you will find this hard to believe. I did this to protect you. Bastille came to me on one my excursions. She said she'd seen you out hunting with your father, and that you were a good shot. Then she told me that she would take you one day, and I would never see you again. I pleaded with her to take me instead of you. I don't know why she agreed to the terms, but she did on the condition I would never return to you.

"I faked my death, dear one, so that you and your father could move on with your life. Yet, I did not trust her agreement, so I became her strongest warrior to gain her trust, to prove my loyalty to her. I wanted to be in the inner circle just in case she captured you anyway. I would never allow her to harm you in anyway. I am sorry I did not have a chance to say goodbye to you."

Alira wipes her eyes and embraces her mother. I reckon all she cares about is having her mother back. The two of them cry happily holding each other after all these years.

Then Michael places a hand on my shoulder. I nod and we walk a few klicks up Route Four. Michael congratulates me for rescuing him. He adds he owes me, but I shake my head. Seeing him smile, having him at my side is all the favor I need.

A little further down Route Four we run into Greg and his gang. It must be Yesh's doing, and even if it isn't I thank him anyway. I introduce Greg to my brother.

Greg offers to drive us back to Brisbane for the small fee of twenty dollars, which Michael happens to have in his wallet.

The gang of bikers drops us off at the hospital and drive off. With all the tossing about, I want to make sure that nothing is broken in Michael or me. While Michael is in with the doctor, I phone our parents.

When I see Mum and Dad in the waiting room, I can't help but latch on to them. Like Alira, I don't want to leave their arms. It seems like we've been away for years when it's only been a few months. I feel like an orphan who suddenly finds her family. Feelings of joy and contentment just mingle all over me so I can't stop smiling.

When the doctor tells Mum and Dad, "One thing I am concerned about is the large bruise on his back," I catch his gaze shift from Mum and Dad. He leans over Michael's shoulder and asks, "How exactly did you get this?"

Considering he was heaved at a stone wall by Zietas, I figure if that's all that's wrong, Michael is surprisingly all right. But I reckon telling the doctor that this giant centipede was angry that Michael kicked him might be too hard to believe.

Michael winces as he takes a breath to tell the doctor some wild, analytical tale. I rush in and say, "If we told you how he acquired all the bruises, you'd probably want to book a session with a shrink."

The doctor strokes his chin in thought then says, "Miss Hauksby, with all I've seen in the news over these past few weeks, your story may not scare me as much as you think it will." He eyes me over his glasses for a moment then says, "But if you would rather keep your little adventure to yourself that's okay by me." He turns to my brother. "Just know you'll feel pain in that area for quite a while. Alternate cold and hot compresses for the next several days. That will help."

Classes resume as normal. We Hauksbys keep the memories of our adventures hidden from most of our schoolies. As far as studies go, we need to take the year again, but so what. Compared to saving Australia from a demonic centipede, I would say one more year of putting up with the blokes of Indro is an anthill.

On my way to my locker, Mr. Tanner stops me in the hall wanting to know about our family trip. I look at him confused. "What family trip? Michael and I never went on a family trip?"

"Travis told me a week ago that he saw your father pulling out of your driveway one morning. When he walked over and asked where you were, your father told him that your mother took you and your brother to the Outback for some bonding time."

I purse my lips. I knew why Dad would tell Travis that, but Travis did not have to yabber to a teacher the whole cover story that Dad conjured up to explain our absence as well as to help him keep his sanity. Yet, Mr. Tanner deserves to know the truth.

"We never went on a trip, sir. Travis had the wrong info. My father probably told him that to cover what we were really doing in the Outback." Mr. Tanner raises an eyebrow. "It's complicated." I know I said I should tell the truth, but would he believe me?

"You were skipping school? I thought you liked history."

"No, it's not that. I love history! I eat it up. It's just you would think I'm troppo if I told you the reason."

"Try me, and we'll see." Something about his manner set me at ease, so I show him.

I pull out the video I took of Zietas when he reared up in the throne room gloating over his new body. Mr. Tanner asks to see the smart phone, so I give it to him and he studies the video. Expressions sweep across his face like ocean waves.

"Either you have some twisted imagination young lady, or a degree in animation or that was one frightful experience!"

"We have the scars and bruises to prove we fought that creature," Mike says walking up.

Mr. Tanner is dumbfounded. He sort of honks when he laughs through his nose. Then he walks back into his classroom honking and muttering. Michael and I look at each other and burst out laughing. We walk down the hall and we run into Travis. I start bumbling apologies at him.

Michael taps me on the shoulder saying, "I'll meet ya outside."

I stare at my feet. Why do I suddenly feel shy around Travis? I never used to feel like this around any bloke at Indro? Then I realize he's acting equally shy around me scuffing his shoe and looking off in the distance instead of at me. Then he pulls the what're-you-doing-this-weekend line. He wants to know if I would like to go see a movie with him.

My guard instantly raises a wall. "Are you asking me out?" I fiddle with my hair asking the question.

"You decide that."

Bursting through the door, Michael says, "Amb, there's someone here I reckon you should see."

Travis gives me a puzzled look, while I follow my brother out. Michael points to the trees at the edge of the field. A figure looks out from behind a tree. A man? I rub my eyes. The man beckons us to come to him. Michael takes a step. Suddenly wary, I clothesline him with my arm. But the man continues to beckon us. Michael and I exchange glances.

"I'm sorry, but I cannot see what the two of you are looking at," Travis says in a baffled tone.

If Travis cannot see the man, then he must be for us, right? I tell Travis to stay put. Then Michael and I cautiously take a step towards the trees. It seems like time stands still. Everyone in the schoolyard slows. Laughter and chatter become a distant murmur. All I see are the trees. Then I see him. A shaman covered with white tribal markings wearing a white loincloth folded on his body like a pair of briefs and a white leather vest. Uli. It has to be. He speaks to us in his native tongue, but fantastically, I understand every word.

"You have done what I could not do, my children. So you have surpassed me in some ways."

"Why couldn't you do it?" My fingers clutch at my throat. I'm confused and enthralled at once. I replied to my grandfather in Wagiman, yet I've never spoken more than a few words in my native tongue! Could it be the power of Yesh? Maybe it is.

Uli confirms it. "It is only natural that you are confused, my child, but it is through Yesh that you are able to understand my words. I am proud of you both. You vanquished the demon and saved this land. You have learned much, and been through much together. Because of this, you are stronger, closer. Both of you looked death in the face as did I. But unlike me, you stood your ground and would not give up. I am sorry I put this yoke on your shoulders. Can you forgive me for running from the task I was meant to accomplish?"

I forgive him outright, but Michael hesitates. I elbow him in the side, so he reluctantly forgives our grandfather as well. Then Grandpa Uli turns to my brother.

"Do not forget your dark time my son," he wisely cautions Michael, "or it will return to tempt you. Remember, how you fell to the temptation to be superior to your sister. That desire may never leave you, but do not entertain it, for that will only bring you pain. Share it with her. Learn your own skills and hone them for she might need your help some day, too."

He bows and then disappears. No goodbyes. No other conversation. He just disappears.

We stand there for just a moment contemplating what we heard then we turn as one walking back together. I see Travis seems to be bursting with curiosity. I squeeze Michael's arm and he nods agreement.

Travis might learn what we did for Australia in time, but for now, I reckon it's best if he remains ignorant. In a way, I envy him. He never saw the horrors we saw. He didn't feel the power of the Centipede's Snare, or succumb to its temptations.

I am sure there will be days when I will wonder if we actually defeated demon. I saw the Centipede fall, but what happened to the demon? Did Mike and I somehow seal up that thylacine-headed monster?

When we walk in our home slinging books on the table, I wonder if Michael pegs it when he says, "It's the first piece moved in a game of chess."